"Do you want the good news or the bad news?"

There was a frown between Andi's brows as she turned to look at Linus. Her inability to think clearly suggested she still hadn't recovered from the freezing cold outside. Or perhaps that was the effect of the whisky. Or, more likely, being held in Linus's arms a few minutes ago....

"The bad news first, I suppose," she invited through lips that tingled painfully with renewed feeling.

Linus nodded. "The bad news is this is just a pub, not a hotel, so the landlord doesn't normally rent out rooms for the night."

Andi blinked. "And the good news...?" she prompted warily.

He grimaced. "He does have a bedroom he can let us use for the night."

Andi moistened her dry lips. "A bedroom, singular...?"

"Bedroom singular," Linus confirmed, his eyes narrowed.

"You aren't suggesting the two of us share that bedroom?"

Carole Mortimer
THE VIRGIN SECRETARY'S IMPOSSIBLE BOSS

International Billionaires

HARLEQUIN®

TORONTO • NEW YORK • LONDON
AMSTERDAM • PARIS • SYDNEY • HAMBURG
STOCKHOLM • ATHENS • TOKYO • MILAN • MADRID
PRAGUE • WARSAW • BUDAPEST • AUCKLAND

Special thanks and acknowledgment
are given to Carole Mortimer for her contribution
to the International Billionaires miniseries.

Recycling programs
for this product may
not exist in your area.

ISBN-13: 978-0-373-23618-3

THE VIRGIN SECRETARY'S IMPOSSIBLE BOSS

First North American Publication 2009.

Copyright © 2009 by Harlequin Books S.A.

www.eHarlequin.com

Printed in U.S.A.

PROLOGUE

'DO WE have a deal?'

Andi stared blankly across the drawing room at the man who had so recently stormed into her own life and her mother's.

'Come on, Andi,' Linus Harrison prompted tersely as he paced impatiently. 'It can't be that difficult for you to realize that you have no real choice but to accept my offer.'

That was the problem. Andi knew she didn't have a choice. And she didn't like it one little bit.

Outwardly her expression and demeanour remained calm. Inwardly it was a different matter. What possible reason could this man have for offering her soon-to-be homeless mother somewhere to live in exchange for Andi taking on the job as his PA? A man like Linus Harrison—a man well-known for his ruthless business reputation, amongst other things—certainly couldn't be making this offer out of the goodness of his heart. Andi wasn't even sure that he had one of those! The hardness of those pale-green eyes set in a harshly sculptured face did nothing to contradict that belief.

Nothing about Linus Harrison, of Harrison Holdings plc, was in the least reassuring, Andi acknowledged as she felt an uncomfortable fluttering in the pit of her stomach just looking at him. He was well over six-feet tall, at least nine or ten inches taller than her own five-feet-four, with over-long, shaggy dark hair that he pushed impatiently from his brow whenever it tumbled forward. His face was as hard and chiselled as any sculpture. Those pale-green eyes. An arrogant slash of a nose above lips that looked as if they rarely smiled. A squarely carved jaw that more than hinted at his ruthless reputation. The tailored dark-grey suit only emphasized the width of his muscled shoulders and tapered waist above long, powerful legs. The whole package was imbued with a restless energy that was in itself overpowering.

Andi drew herself up to her full height of five feet six inches—in two-inch heels—none of her inner disquiet showing as she looked at Linus Harrison with calm brown eyes. 'My name is Miss Buttonfield, or Andrea, if you prefer. Only my family and close friends are invited to use the familiarity of "Andi".' She raised challenging blonde brows.

Linus's expression was mocking as his gaze swept over her admiringly. Andrea Buttonfield had class with a capital C!

She was nine years younger than his own thirty-five years. The top of her blonde head barely reached his chin. Her straight, shoulder-length hair was expertly styled, the fringe feathering lightly above huge eyes the colour of rich, dark chocolate. There were dark shadows beneath those beautiful eyes. Her cheeks were slightly hollow, her nose small and straight, and her mouth a perfect bow above a stubbornly pointed chin. Her cool, businesslike appearance was completed by a tailored black skirt and white silk blouse.

In the last three months this woman had been hit with one tragedy on top of another, and yet Linus could see only cool determination in those liquid brown eyes as she continued to look at him unblinkingly.

Linus gave a taunting inclination of his head. 'In that case, I'll settle for Andrea. For now,' he drawled derisively. 'I should warn you that I'm not a patient man, Andrea,' he added harshly. 'My offer is only open until five o'clock today.'

The slight widening of those brown eyes was her only outward response to his ultimatum.

He shrugged. 'It's the way I do business, *Andrea.*'

She shook her head. 'I can't possibly make such a life-changing decision in just a few hours.'

'That will be your loss.'

A frown darkened her creamy brow. 'Why the hurry?'

'My present PA is leaving at the end of the month and I need a replacement before that happens.' Linus moved to lower his long length into one of the gold-brocade armchairs that adorned the perfection of the spacious drawing-room.

As Linus already knew, every room in Tarrington Park was decorated and furnished in this same gracious, elegant style. It was a style that Linus wanted to keep when he took possession of Tarrington Park in several weeks' time and turned it into another of his luxury spa-hotels and conference centres. It was a style that Marjorie Buttonfield, Andi's mother, had informed Linus was all her daughter's own work.

Style—that was the word that applied to everything about Andrea Buttonfield. Not surprisingly. Andi had grown up on the Tarrington Park estate, the only child of Miles and Marjorie Buttonfield. Her childhood had been one of luxury and indulgence. Her private boarding-schools were the best in the country. Her English degree from Cambridge university was one of the highest attainable. Following university, Andrea had moved to live in London, becoming the PA of Gerald Wickham, head of Wickham International.

Yes, Andrea Buttonfield had style.

Linus's own childhood and education was the complete opposite of Andi's, and it was her style and class he had coveted from the moment he'd first met her eight weeks ago, when he'd come to look over Tarrington Park with the intention of buying it.

Andrea's father had been killed in a car accident four weeks earlier, along with her fiancé, David Simmington-Browne. The following weeks had revealed that, not only was her father's company bankrupt, but there were considerable debts too. Selling the family home had become the only solution to paying off those debts.

Linus had done his homework on Tarrington

Park, Andrea and the recently widowed Marjorie Buttonfield. He knew selling the family home would leave the already grief-stricken Marjorie homeless and without any means of support other than the wage her daughter earnt as Wickham's PA.

It was a chink in Andrea Buttonfield's armour that Linus didn't hesitate to use to his own advantage.

'Think about it, Andrea.' Linus smiled humourlessly. 'As my PA, you'll get an increase in wages. You and your mother get to move into the gate house, which as well as being rent-free has to be less traumatic for the both of you. You could continue to keep your horse at the stables here. As far as you're concerned, it's a win-win situation.'

Andi was already well aware of all the pluses of accepting Linus Harrison's offer. It was the minuses that concerned her. She didn't know Linus Harrison. She didn't trust Linus Harrison. Most of all, she didn't *like* Linus Harrison!

His well-earned reputation for ruthlessness in business didn't give the impression that he ever did things impulsively, telling Andi that he must have given this offer a lot of thought before making it. 'And what do you get out of it, Mr Harrison?' she prompted shrewdly.

'In Gerald Wickham's opinion, the best PA in the western hemisphere!' Those green eyes openly mocked her.

Andi's own eyes widened incredulously. 'You've already spoken to Gerald about me?' That was how he knew that the money he was offering her was an increase…!

Linus Harrison shrugged wide shoulders. 'I would hardly consider taking you on as my own PA without first talking to your previous employer.'

'My *current* employer!' Andi corrected with an impatient shake of her head as she glared at him. 'You had absolutely no right to talk to Gerald.'

'I had every right,' Linus Harrison cut in coldly, those eyes hard. 'I would no more consider employing someone because she looks the part than I would consider buying a car just because it has sleek lines!'

Her mouth thinned. 'I'm not sure whether that was an insult or a compliment!'

'It was a statement of fact,' Linus rasped. 'For all I knew, you could be lousy at your job and just sleeping with Gerald Wickham to keep it!'

It was a possibility that hadn't found any favour in Linus's eyes, and definitely detracted from that style and class Andrea Buttonfield possessed in spades. Admittedly, until three months ago Andrea had been engaged to Simmington-Browne. But that didn't mean she wasn't also sleeping with her boss. One meeting with Gerald Wickham had convinced Linus that the other man thought of Andrea in the way an indulgent uncle might a favourite niece, rather than an expensive mistress reserved for his physical pleasure.

Why that information should have mattered to Linus he had no idea. Admittedly, his own code of conduct concerning female employees dictated he not become personally involved with any of them, but he knew that a lot of men in his position didn't feel the same way.

Andi didn't know whether to be furious or just indignant at the familiarity of this man's conversation. She decided that disdain probably suited the occasion better. 'I presume Gerald satisfied your curiosity on that score?'

'Totally,' Linus Harrison confirmed.

Andi eyed him frustratedly. 'I am more than happy with my present employment, Mr Harrison. My mother has been offered a cottage in the village to live in. And one of the local livery-stables has agreed to take my horse. So you see, Mr Harrison—'

'As I said, I have no use for the gate house, so it would be rent-free. Your horse would also be stabled free of charge. Plus,' he continued before Andi could interrupt, 'do you really think that your mother's already-delicate emotional health is up to moving into a cottage in the village where your family has long been considered the local gentry?'

Andi became very still. The car accident that had killed both Andi's father and her fiancé had seemed an almost unbearable blow at the time; initially only the necessity to keep focused for her mother's sake had held Andi's own grief in check. The revelation only days later of the bankruptcy of her father's company was a blow Andi certainly hadn't been expecting.

Her mother hadn't coped well; the loss of her husband of thirty years, quickly followed by the knowledge that she was shortly to lose her home as well, had left Marjorie balancing on a very precarious mental edge. One more blow and Andi knew her mother was likely to topple over into the precipice.

As it was, these last weeks had been a nightmare as Andi had tried to balance visits to her mother at the weekends and her demanding job in London as Gerald's PA during the week. It was a strain that Andi knew was beginning to take its toll on her after three months, both emotionally and physically.

The truth of the matter was, her mother would be much happier if Andi moved back to live with her in Hampshire, especially if she was also allowed to stay in the gate house of Tarrington Park. Andi would feel happier knowing that her mother was comfortable. It was only the thought of becoming Linus Harrison's PA that stopped Andi from jumping at the opportunity he was offering her.

That, and the fact that she simply didn't like or trust him.

She felt distinctly uncomfortable in Linus Harrison's presence. She already knew that this man didn't just look like an iceberg but had the characteristic of one too.

Andi looked at him frostily. 'I'm not sure I want to work for a man who uses another person's weakness in order to get what he wants.'

He gave a mocking smile. 'I don't think it was part of the job description that you actually have to like me!'

'Perhaps as well,' Andi drawled derisively. 'Could you tell me what that job description *does* entail?'

Linus gave a dismissive shrug. 'Obviously, all the duties you have at the moment. Plus, once the work starts, we'll be spending most of our time here for at least the next year working on the transformation of Tarrington Park into one of Harrison Holdings' most prestigious hotels and conference centres. I'll need to go up to my office in London occasionally, as well as giving a certain amount of time to visiting my other hotels. But for the main part I like to work on a hands-on basis, overseeing every detail of the building alterations myself.

'Not that there should be too many of those, when this house already lends itself to what I have in mind. The décor is something I would like you to deal with. I usually hire a team in London, but you know this house better than anyone. Your input is going to be invaluable once it comes to furnishing and decorating the rooms in a style that complements its amenities. With your help, I hope, *Andrea*, Tarrington Park is going to become the most luxurious spa-hotel and conference centre in the country.'

Andi felt a fluttering of excitement as Linus Harrison outlined his plans for her childhood home. Of course she would have preferred that they didn't have to sell Tarrington Park at all, that her mother could just be allowed to continue living here, but Andi knew after the last few months that that was impossible. With the sale of Tarrington Park they would be able to pay off her father's debts, and, although Linus Harrison was possibly the last person Andi would ever have wanted to sell it to, his offer of employment meant she would at least be able to have a say in the alternations and the décor. Her mother would be able to remain on the estate too, albeit in the much smaller gate house rather than the manor-house itself.

Linus easily read the wavering resolve in Andi's expression. 'Admit it, Andrea—you're tempted by the idea,' he taunted.

Her eyes flashed darkly. 'The *idea* maybe,' she allowed waspishly. 'The reality is a different matter. I'm really not sure I could work for you.'

His gaze narrowed. 'Why the hell not? No, let me guess,' he continued harshly. 'Someone with your privileged background shudders at the mere idea of being employed by someone like me!'

She blinked. 'Someone "like you"…?'

'I'm sure you, like every other reader of tabloid newspapers, are aware of my background,' Linus rasped knowingly.

The press had made much, over the years, of

the fact that Linus had started out with nothing fifteen years ago but the sharpness of his brain and a determination to succeed. That, although he was a multi-millionaire now, he had started out as the only child of a single mother, brought up in the back streets of Glasgow, leaving school at the age of sixteen to work as a labourer on a building site.

Within four years he owned his own building company, buying run-down properties and turning them into hotels, each one more luxurious than the next. Until now, fifteen years later, Linus owned dozens of them all over the world.

Along the way he had lost his Glaswegian accent, learnt to wear Armani suits as if born to it, and had become as comfortable in the company of lords and ladies as he was with his own labourers.

Andrea Buttonfield looked confused by his accusatory tone. 'Why should your background matter to me?'

Why indeed? Linus instantly berated himself for revealing even this much of a chink in his own armour. As far as Andrea Buttonfield was concerned, she had reason enough to dislike him simply because he was the upstart who intended to buy her family home and turn it into a profitable business-venture. For her, he could now see, the added knowledge that their backgrounds were so dissimilar simply didn't come into the equation.

Some of the tension left his shoulders, although the restless anger remained. 'I've decided I don't want to wait for your decision after all, Andrea,' Linus bit out impatiently. 'What's it to be? Take it or leave it.'

Andi wanted to leave it. Every instinct in her body told her to do exactly that. But just the thought of how her mother had changed these last three months—of the fragility of her emotional state, let alone her mental one—was enough to give Andi pause for thought.

Linus Harrison's offer of employment would solve so many problems for her concerning her mother. Andi knew she would be a fool to turn down that offer just because being in the same room with Linus Harrison made her feel so uneasy.

She drew in a deeply controlled breath. 'Okay; I accept your offer, Mr Harrison. But my contract says I have to give Gerald three months' notice, not one,' she added determinedly as she saw the brief triumph that blazed in those beautiful eyes.

Linus Harrison looked completely unperturbed. 'I can live with that.'

Andi just hoped that *she* could live with the ramifications of her decision...

CHAPTER ONE

'PACK your bags, Andi, we're going to Scotland for a few days!'

Andi looked up, frowning, to where Linus stood in the doorway that separated their two offices on the top floor of Tarrington Park. She had already known he was here at his private apartments just down the hallway from their offices, having seen his car parked out on the forecourt when she'd arrived for work this morning. It was what he had said that caused her to react so sharply. 'Scotland?'

'Hmm.' Linus strode further into the room to lean against the side of her desk. His dark hair was styled only slightly shorter than it had been a year ago; the pale green of his eyes was still as icily astute in the rugged handsomeness of his hard, chiselled features as he looked down at her. 'Now that Tarrington Park has opened, I'm looking for another big project to work on. There's a castle in Scotland I'm thinking of buying.'

Andi eyed him. 'And you want me to go with you?' He had never suggested taking her away on business with him before. He hadn't suggested it now, either, Andi reminded herself derisively—Linus had *told* her they were going.

'You are my PA,' he reminded her.

Andi was well aware of what she was. Just as she was aware that during the last few months she had started to see Linus as more than just the demanding employer who would appear for a few chaotic days to check on progress at Tarrington Park, and then just as abruptly disappear back to his life and apartment in London.

Expecting Andi to accompany him to Scotland on business was a perfectly reasonable request for Linus to make of his PA. In fact, when Andi had worked for Gerald Wickham, she had gone away on business with him all the time. But Linus wasn't Gerald…

Totally aware of Linus's ruthless reputation when it came to women as well as business, Andi had been determined to keep him safely at arm's length when she'd begun working for him a year ago. Not difficult to do when she still felt so emotionally numb following the deaths of David and her father.

But gradually—insidiously, it seemed—Andi had found herself looking forward to Linus's whirlwind visits. She had become aware of the sexy seductiveness of Linus's pale eyes; the wolfishness of his rare smile. She had come to appreciate the width of his shoulders and leanness of his muscled body as he strode forcefully through Tarrington Park issuing orders that he would expect to have carried out by his next visit.

Just as Andi was now totally and heatedly aware of his close proximity as he leant against the side of her desk.

Andi gave a self-disgusted grimace as she pulled her laptop towards her. 'Which airport are we flying to?' she prompted briskly, thankfully able to breathe a little easier as Linus stood up and moved away slightly.

'I thought I might drive up in the Range Rover.'

'Drive?' Andi glanced out of the window at the bleakness of the winter sky. 'Doesn't it snow in Scotland in February?'

'Stop being picky, Andi,' Linus rasped dismissively. 'Anyone would think you don't want to go to Scotland with me.'

That was because she didn't!

Just the thought of being alone in Scotland with Linus for several days, when she was now so physically aware of him, made her stomach-muscles clench and her pulse race.

He scowled down at her. 'What is your problem, Andi? Do you have other plans for this weekend? A romantic tryst, perhaps?' he added mockingly.

'Of course not,' she snapped.

Linus gave a taunting smile. 'Of course not,' he parroted derisively. 'It's been over a year since the saintly David Simmington-Browne died, so isn't it time you started living again?' Especially as her fiancé really hadn't been that saintly, Linus acknowledged disgustedly. He had unfortunately found out far too many of the other man's secrets in the last year. Secrets he knew Andi was totally unaware of…

His decision to make Andrea Buttonfield his on-site PA, and give her a free hand when it came to the interior of Tarrington Park, had been the best business move he'd ever made, Linus acknowledged ruefully. But the newly renovated hotel and conference centre had been open for a month now, managed very successfully by Michael Hall, and it was time to move on to something else. For both of them.

Andi had stiffened at Linus's remark about David. 'My private life is none of your concern.' Her tone was frosty.

Linus gave a disgusted snort. 'You don't *have* a private life.'

'Then it's just as well you have enough of one for both of us, isn't it?' Andi gave him a scathing glance, knowing from the photographs that often appeared in the newspapers that Linus's life in London involved evenings, if not nights, with the latest woman in his life. Women who rarely engaged his interest longer than a couple of months.

Linus raised mocking brows. 'Jealous?'

Andi stiffened. 'Certainly not!' she gasped, even as she felt the heated colour enter her cheeks.

She wasn't jealous of those women in Linus's life. In fact, Andi found her own awareness of him totally confusing. David had been smoothly charming; suave and sophisticated. Linus possessed charm and sophistication when he chose to, but his attraction was raw. Sexual, sensuous, earthy…

She stood up abruptly. 'What is there for me to feel jealous of?' she scorned. 'If those women are stupid enough to accept the little you want to give them, then that's their problem. I can assure you that I have absolutely no interest in warming your bed!' Andi regretted the words almost as soon as she had said them, realizing she might have said too much. Revealed too much.

Linus regarded Andi through narrowed lids, inwardly surprised by her vehemence. He only came to Tarrington Park every couple of months, but never during any of those visits had he seen the coolly distant Andi this rattled by anything; those gorgeous brown eyes were positively gleaming with her indignation, and bright spots of angry colour were on her usually pale cheeks.

His mouth hardened. 'Maybe you should wait until you're asked before saying no,' he teased. 'I was referring to your own lack of a love-life just now, Andi,' he explained.

She blinked, her polite, businesslike mask falling back into place as she resumed her seat behind the desk. 'I knew that,' she dismissed sharply.

Linus continued to look at her for several long seconds, contemplating Andi's completely defensive reaction.

Things had been a little tense between the

two of them when they'd first begun working together, probably due to a certain amount of understandable resentment on Andi's part at almost being bullied into working for him. But once Andi had accepted that Linus genuinely did want her complete input into the renovations to Tarrington Park—and that his long absences gave her a free rein when it came to the inner décor, the awkwardness between them had started to fade. Now, a year later, Linus totally appreciated that when it came to his business affairs Andi was quiet, efficient and everything that he could wish for in a PA.

Her reaction just now reminded him that she was also an extremely beautiful woman. The tailored suits and blouses she always wore could never hide the fact that she was shapely in all the right places, with long, sexy legs that went all the way up to her…

'Linus?'

'Sorry.' He gave an impatient shake of his head as he brought his wandering thoughts back from considering just how sexily attractive his PA was. 'We'll start the drive up to Scotland tomorrow,' he bit out abruptly as he straightened. 'Besides viewing the castle near Edinburgh, there's someone I need to visit.'

'Edinburgh?' Andi echoed. 'Just a moment.' She eyed him suspiciously. 'Isn't the Scottish rugby team playing against Wales over the weekend?'

'I think that they are, yes,' Linus confirmed lightly, his expression deliberately innocent.

'You *think* that they are,' Andi echoed knowingly.

She knew that Linus didn't just like to play hard, but that his business success was due to the fact that he worked like a fiend too. But, no matter how wealthy he had become, or how busy he was, Linus had maintained his boyhood love for the game of rugby, and whenever possible he attended the games played by the Scottish team.

It was impossible to miss the fact that the Six Nations tournament was about to start this weekend, or that Scotland were due to play at home at Murrayfield, an area of Edinburgh, on Sunday. Too much of a coincidence in the circumstances.

'You know that they are, Linus.' Andi gave a derisive shake of her head. 'In fact, I bet you have a ticket for the game.' She raised mocking brows.

'Actually, I have two tickets,' he conceded dryly.

Andi's eyes widened. 'You're expecting me to go to a rugby match with you too?'

He scowled. 'Why not?'

For one thing, Andi had absolutely no interest in the game of rugby. For another, attending a rugby match with Linus certainly wasn't in her job description.

Andi shrugged. 'If you're visiting friends and going to a rugby match I really don't see why you need me with you in Scotland at all.'

Linus's scowl darkened ominously. 'This is the first time I've asked you to come away on business with me and you're refusing?'

'I didn't say that.' She shook her head slowly, aware of that dangerous glitter in Linus's eyes.

'That's what it sounded like to me,' he rasped tersely.

'Then you must have misheard,' Andi came back calmly.

Had he? Linus wondered, frowning. He and Andi had worked well together on the occasions he'd come to Tarrington Park, but on a personal level they had never got past the stage of his being allowed to call her 'Andi', instead of the 'Andrea' she had initially insisted upon. A situation that Linus had thought suited them both, until Andi's sharp response just now…

He frowned darkly. 'Are you coming to Scotland with me or not?'

Andi gave a cool inclination of her head. 'Of course I will accompany you, if that's what you want.'

'What I want from you, Andi, is your input on the castle near Edinburgh. You did a good job with Tarrington Park; I could use your help,' he stated clearly. 'Will Marjorie be okay left on her own for four days?'

'She isn't on her own any more since you employed Mrs Ferguson as our housekeeper,' Andi reminded him waspishly.

Linus scowled impatiently. 'Don't tell me you're still annoyed about that?'

Andi had been more than a little put out when, during one of his whirlwind visits to Tarrington Park six months ago, Linus had calmly informed her that he had hired a housekeeper for the gate house. Not that it didn't make a lot of sense to have someone taking care of the house; Andi just didn't like feeling any more in Linus's debt than she already was.

Her mother's health was much improved from a year ago. The scandal of bankruptcy that had been revealed following Miles's death had died down eventually, allowing Marjorie to pull back from that emotional edge she had been teetering on—although her mother was still more delicate than Andi would have liked.

But her mother and Mrs Ferguson were of a similar age and got on very well together, meaning there was absolutely no need for Andi to be in the least concerned about leaving Marjorie for a few days. 'I wasn't annoyed,' she assured Linus frostily. 'I just wish you had consulted me before you did it, that's all.'

'If I had, you would only have said no; I decided not to put us both through that particular argument.' He dismissed her with his usual arrogance. 'I keep you pretty busy here, and the gate house is far too big for your mother to manage on her own.'

'Don't bother trying to explain, Linus.' Andi sighed. 'We both know that in my mother's eyes you can do no wrong.'

He raised dark brows. 'What can I say? Women of a certain age seem to like me.'

It had come as something of a surprise to Andi that Linus chose to visit her mother whenever he came to Tarrington Park. His manner towards Marjorie was always warm and considerate. The fact that he had watched his own mother struggle to bring him up alone perhaps answered some of his softer feelings towards her mother. Whatever Linus's reasons, he seemed to have a genuine affection for Marjorie, and she was constantly singing his praises.

Andi's mouth twisted. 'The newspapers seem to think it's women in general!'

'Oh, give it a rest, Andi.' He gave her an irritated frown. 'You can't deny that employing Mrs Ferguson has made things easier for Marjorie.'

'I'm not denying anything.' Andi gave him a considering look. 'Is life always that easy for you—something isn't quite right, so throw some money at it and fix it?'

Brought up at Tarrington Park, surrounded by the indulgent love of both her parents, Andi couldn't even begin to imagine what life had been like for Linus as a child, or a teenager. There had been lots of love—initially from his mother, and then from his Aunt Mae after his mother's death when he was fifteen. But there certainly hadn't been any money to spend on 'fixing' anything. It was one of the perks of his now considerable wealth that Linus could buy anything he pleased; could do what he wanted when he wanted. And usually did…

Andi had never complained about the long

hours she had to work to bring about the changes in Tarrington Park, but Linus had been aware on his brief visits that she worried about her mother being left on her own so much. It had been easy for Linus to solve that problem by hiring a housekeeper. The way Andi had reacted at the time, anyone would have thought *he*'d been trying to move into the gate house with her!

'It's not always about money, Andrea,' he conceded dryly. 'But nothing I seem to do or say stops you from being stubbornly argumentative.'

Colour heightened the hollows of her cheeks. 'I'm independent, Linus, not stubborn. There is a difference, you know.'

His mouth thinned. 'Could you afford to take on a housekeeper?'

'You know that I couldn't.'

'Then stop complaining because I could! It seemed the right time, especially with the new development in Scotland.'

'Linus, you aren't actually expecting me to move to Edinburgh to oversee the renovations if you buy this castle, are you?' Andi gasped as the idea occurred to her, her expression one of horrified disbelief at the prospect.

'Of course I'm not expecting you to move to Scotland,' Linus taunted. 'Live there for several weeks at a time, maybe, but not actually move there.' He looked at her challengingly.

Andi stared at him. 'Is that the real reason you employed Mrs Ferguson?'

His mouth thinned. 'What are you talking about?'

Andi grimaced. 'You employed Mrs Ferguson because you knew that once Tarrington Park had opened my full-time presence would no longer be needed here.'

'Did I?' Linus's voice was dangerously soft.

'Of course!'

'Andi, I have no idea what I've done to give you the impression that my every act is Machiavellian in nature.'

'Why don't we start with the fact that you bullied me into working for you?'

'That can change any time you feel like resigning!' Linus assured her icily.

Andi frowned at him. Their two gazes were locked in a battle of wills, her own accusing, Linus's challenging.

Andi's gaze was the first to drop. 'Do you want me to book the hotel in Edinburgh for all three nights?' she prompted stiffly.

'We aren't staying at a hotel any of the nights,' Linus informed her tersely. 'I've made my own arrangements,' he added playfully as Andi raised questioning brows.

She shrugged. 'I'll need to know where we're staying so that I can let my mother know where I am.'

He nodded abruptly, obviously still annoyed about her earlier accusation of duplicity. 'We will be staying at my Aunt Mae's, near Ayr, tomorrow night. Then I've arranged—'

'At your Aunt Mae's…?' Andi repeated, with a sinking feeling in the pit of her stomach.

Linus raised arrogant brows. 'You have a problem with that?'

Not a problem, exactly. More a reservation. It was easy enough for Andi to keep her emotional distance from Linus on the visits he made to Tarrington Park, when she dealt with him only in a business capacity. Actually staying with him at the home of one of his relatives was far too intimate for comfort—Andi's comfort.

She shook her head. 'I'm sure your aunt won't want one of your employees intruding on your visit.'

'On the contrary,' Linus drawled derisively, 'She's looking forward to meeting you.'

Andi's eyes widened. 'She is?'

'Oh yes.' He nodded mockingly. 'She very

much wants to meet the woman who has managed to put up with me for the last year.'

'As your employee, you mean?' Andi croaked.

'Of course as my employee,' Linus acknowledged tauntingly, those amazing eyes openly mocking. 'The previous record for being my PA was only ten months.'

'I didn't know that...' Andi's voice tailed off. Admittedly Linus's work schedule was as demanding as he was, the hours long, meaning that Andi's hours often were too. But she couldn't deny that she had found the last year completely absorbing, culminating in a strong feeling of satisfaction when Tarrington Park had finally opened as a hotel and conference centre, becoming almost an overnight success.

Linus shrugged. 'I didn't think it was important!'

'Exactly what did you do to my predecessors?' she questioned dryly.

'Absolutely nothing,' he bit out harshly.

'Ah.' Andi nodded slowly, her stomach muscles tightening. 'I take it that was the problem?'

'Apparently.' He nodded tersely. 'I don't get involved with the women who work for me, Andi,' he added abruptly.

Andi had a sick feeling in the pit of her

stomach. She wondered if she had somehow given away her increasing awareness of Linus as a dangerously attractive man. Maybe this was his way of warning her not even to contemplate any thoughts of an intimate relationship ever developing between the two of them.

'Then it's lucky for both of us that I have absolutely no interest whatsoever in pursuing a relationship with you out of the office!' she came back coldly.

Linus wouldn't have called it lucky, exactly; Andi really was an extraordinarily beautiful woman. But by making Andi his employee Linus had effectively put an end to the idea of anything of a personal nature ever developing between the two of them.

Although, he couldn't deny that his interest had been piqued a few minutes ago when Andi had reacted so defensively to the mere suggestion of intimacy between the two of them— before she had insulted him concerning his employment of Mrs Ferguson.

'Lucky for both of us,' he rasped dismissively.

Andi nodded. 'By the way, Linus,' she added challengingly as he went to go through to the adjoining office. 'Perhaps I should just mention that my maternal grandfather is Welsh.'

He winced. 'Does that mean you'll be cheering for Wales at the game on Sunday?'

Andi gave him a sunny smile. 'It certainly does. They have a good record, I believe?'

Linus gave her a considering look. 'You know more about the game than I thought,' he finally murmured.

'Not really.' She grimaced. 'I just remember all of my grandfather's telephone calls when they win a game.'

'Hmm.' Linus frowned. 'After ten years, it's time for Scotland to win again.'

'Or England. They're playing Italy on Saturday, I believe?' she added innocently.

He gave a low groan. 'I can see we're going to have fun this weekend.'

Andi wasn't sure that 'fun' was how she viewed the prospect of the next four days, being alone in Scotland with Linus. Totally physically aware of him as she was, and warned off by Linus's claim that he never became involved with female employees, those four days promised to be difficult in the extreme…

CHAPTER TWO

'I THOUGHT you said it didn't always snow in Scotland in February.'

'Okay, so it turns out I was wrong.' Linus scowled darkly as he sat behind the wheel of the Range Rover, trying to see the road ahead through the heavily falling snow.

They had set out from Hampshire very early that morning, stopping off somewhere near Manchester for lunch before continuing the drive. It was dark as the snow began to fall softly almost as soon as they drove over the border between England and Scotland, that snow becoming heavier the further they drove towards his aunt's home near Ayr, on the west coast.

'Perhaps you should have checked the weather forecast before we set out,' he added impatiently.

'*I* should have? You gave me the impression that you had everything about this trip under control,' Andi murmured dryly, no more happy at the possibility of having to come to Scotland for weeks at a time than she had been yesterday when she'd first realized it was a possibility.

'Unfortunately, even I can't control the weather!' It really was foul, Linus acknowledged grimly as it occurred to him he could see barely six feet in front. Their progress was becoming slower by the minute. 'If it doesn't let up soon, then we may have to look for somewhere else to stay for the night.'

He could feel Andi's gaze on him as she gave him a sharp look.

'Is it really that bad?'

'You can see that for yourself.' He nodded in the direction of the road ahead. The grass verge and the road were hardly distinguishable from each other now; the road itself was rapidly being covered in a treacherous layer of slippery snow.

Not that the Range Rover wasn't up to dealing with it, but it was no good if Linus couldn't see where he was going. The fact that he hadn't seen any traffic coming down the road the other way for some time now told him that the way ahead was probably even worse than it was here.

'I have no intention of sleeping in the Range Rover, so look out for somewhere we can stop for the night.' Linus grimly kept his concentration on the road in front of them.

Andi turned her attention to looking through the falling snow for any sign of habitation, especially for the lights of an inn or a hotel where they could rest until the snow eased. She felt overwhelmingly guilty because she hadn't checked the weather forecast and wasn't more prepared. Feeling disgruntled with Linus over the possibility of having to live in Scotland for weeks at a time was really no excuse.

'Over there!' she suddenly cried, pointing to a light ahead of them on the left-hand side of the road. 'It could be an inn, or— No, it's just a street lamp.' She grimaced her disappointment.

'A street lamp has to mean habitation of some kind.' Linus narrowed his gaze in the direction she had pointed. 'Yes! A short way down that lane—at least, I hope it's a lane.' He frowned darkly as he turned the vehicle in the direction of the lights, the covering of snow obscuring everything but a flat blanket of white that he sincerely hoped had some sort of firm surface beneath. 'It's an inn,' Linus added with satisfaction as he saw the sign, bearing a thistle and a stag, swinging in the gusting wind. He turned the Range Rover into what he hoped was the otherwise deserted car-park, easing the tension in his shoulders as he gently put on the brakes and brought the vehicle to a stop. 'Not a very big inn, but it will have to do.' He grimaced out of the window at the small, barely discernible building. 'Feel like making a run for it?' Ruefully, he turned to prompt Andi.

She grimaced. 'Do we have any other choice?'

'No—but I thought I would ask anyway,' Linus baited her as he reached in the back of the vehicle to get their coats, handing Andi's to her before pulling on his own. 'Don't get out until I come round for you,' he advised firmly as he braced himself for opening the door and facing the freezing weather outside. 'If I lose you in this, I might never find you again!'

Andi shivered as she felt the blast of ice-cold wind when Linus quickly opened the door and climbed out, before closing it again. The snow was falling so thickly now that she couldn't even see him as he made his way round the vehicle to her side; she was only aware that he had done so when the door was wrenched open beside her.

It had only been a few seconds, but Linus was already covered in snow, his coat hidden beneath the icy flakes, the darkness of his hair bearing a frosting of the fluffy whiteness too. 'Careful; it's icy,' he warned as Andi lowered her feet to the ground.

His warning came a little too late as her feet slipped from under her and she had to reach out quickly to grasp the front of Linus's coat to stop herself from falling. 'Sorry,' she muttered between gritted teeth as she tried to steady herself. The wind and snow were so icy-cold that her face and jaw already felt frozen, her hair whipping about her face in wet tangles. 'This is terrible!' she attempted to shout above the roar of the wind, knowing Linus hadn't heard her as he gave an irritated shake of his head, dislodging some of the snow in his hair so that it dripped down the grimness of his face and quickly melted against the heat of his skin.

Linus took a firm hold of her hand and turned to fight against the wind as they began to struggle towards the inn. The going was slow, and Andi was surprised at how far away it still looked when she glanced up, the icy wind beating against them so remorselessly that it seemed to deliberately hinder their progress. Almost as if it didn't want them to reach the shelter and warmth the inn promised.

Andi couldn't breathe properly through her

nose, her throat burning when she attempted to breathe through her mouth instead. All the time the snow beat against her face, hard and painful as it stung against her flesh.

'Damn it, we're getting nowhere like this!' She barely heard Linus's impatient exclamation before it was carried away on the howling wind, so she was totally unprepared when Linus turned to swing her up into his arms and hold her close against his chest as he walked more determinedly towards the lights of the inn.

Andi's arms were thrown about his neck as she burrowed her face against him to shelter from the icy-cold wind. Even the dampness of his coat was more comfortable than the burning in her throat as she tried to breathe through that frosty battering.

Incredible to think that, although it had been cold, the sun had actually been trying to shine when they'd left Hampshire earlier this morning; it was like being in another world.

What would happen to them if Linus couldn't make it as far as the inn? Her arms tightened about Linus's neck as she laced her frozen fingers tightly together. She should have thought to wear gloves. And a hat.

'Almost there!' Linus rasped grimly, obviously suffering as much as she was from the wind that was so cold it seemed to rip right through them. 'Get the door,' he prompted forcefully seconds later.

Andi raised her head and saw that they had actually reached the inn; light shone welcomingly through the small, frosted windows, and what looked like the warm glow of a fire too.

Her fingers were so cold, so numbed, that she had trouble unlacing them. The snow cracked on the sleeve of her coat and then fell away as she moved her arm towards the doorknob, fingers slipping at first before she managed to grasp and turn it. The two of them almost fell through the open doorway straight into what looked like the public bar.

Much to the incredulity of the landlord, as he gazed across at them with disbelieving eyes, his mouth having fallen open in surprise at anyone being out at all on an evening like this.

'Shut the door behind us, would you?' Linus instructed the other man grimly as he carried Andi over to where a fire burned warmly in the hearth in the otherwise deserted bar. He sat down, still holding Andi against him, as she seemed unable to release her clenched fingers from the shoulders of his jacket, her teeth chattering uncontrollably.

'It's okay, Andi,' he murmured reassuringly. 'We're okay,' he added with satisfaction as the warmth of the fire began to thaw his numbed face and hands.

The tingling sensation that ensued was almost as painful, but it was a welcome pain after the worry of the last few minutes. He really hadn't been sure they were going to make it as far as the inn as the snowstorm had become a blizzard, visibility down to almost nil, each step becoming a triumph of survival.

Not that Linus intended telling Andi that. He knew from experience that Andi was a woman who usually remained calm in any situation; she had through the death of her father and fiancé, the selling of her family home to pay off her father's debts and coming to work for him. But the way she still clung to him so tightly now showed she had definitely reached the end of her endurance.

Arousingly so, Linus realized as he looked down at her with narrowed green eyes. She looked so tiny in his arms, vulnerable, even, her hair plastered to her head and across her face in damp tendrils, her eyes huge as she raised her head to look at him. A man could willingly drown in those chocolate-brown depths, Linus realized with a sharp intake of breath; could lose his own will, his very soul, and not give a damn as long as Andi continued to look up at him with that warmth in her eyes.

He had never noticed before how long her lashes were, thick and dark, a beguiling contrast to the honey-blonde of her hair. Her lips were a deep pink, full and pouting, as if waiting to be kissed.

'Get the other side of this, lad. And your good lady, too.'

Linus wrenched his gaze away from Andi to look at the landlord as he stood beside the armchair holding two glasses of amber liquid. Probably whisky, Linus acknowledged ruefully as he gratefully took one of the glasses and held the rim next to Andi's lips. 'Drink,' he instructed firmly as she made no effort to do so.

Andi's throat moved convulsively as she acknowledged that there was something in Linus's eyes just now as he looked down at her, an awareness that only increased her own wariness about spending these four days alone with him in Scotland.

She obediently sipped the golden liquid, almost choking on the unaccustomed alcohol as the whisky slid down her throat to burst into a fiery warmth as it reached her stomach, warming her from the inside out. Thawing Andi enough for her to realize she was sitting on Linus's thighs and still cradled in his arms.

She struggled to sit up, taking the glass of whisky from his hand as she stood up and moved sharply away from him, averting her face to stare into the fire as she sensed his questioning gaze following her movements.

What had happened just now?

She had looked up into Linus's face and seen—what? Awareness, certainly. Desire, possibly. Almost as if Linus had been looking at her for the first time. And perhaps he had. Andi certainly bore little resemblance today to the prim no-nonsense PA she chose to present to him in the office. Her hair fell loosely about her shoulders; her denims and jumper were much more casual than anything she would ever wear to the office. She felt strangely vulnerable without the shield of her tailored business-suits and blouses. Especially if that change had also affected the way Linus viewed her.

She suddenly became aware of the conversation taking place between Linus and the landlord.

'Get my wife to make up the room,' the

landlord murmured before hurrying away and disappearing through a door marked 'private'.

'Do you want the good news or the bad news?'

There was a frown between Andi's brows as she turned to look at Linus, her inability to think clearly telling her that she still hadn't recovered from the freezing cold outside. Or perhaps that was the effect of the whisky. Or, more likely, being held in Linus's arms a few minutes ago…

'The bad news first, I suppose,' she invited through lips that tingled painfully with renewed feeling.

Linus nodded. 'The bad news is this is just a pub, not a hotel, so the landlord doesn't normally rent out rooms for the night.'

Andi blinked. 'And the good news…?' she prompted warily.

He grimaced. 'He does have a bedroom he can let us use for the night. It's his daughter's bedroom, but she's away at university at the moment.'

Andi moistened dry lips. '*A* bedroom— singular…?'

'Bedroom, singular,' Linus confirmed, his eyes narrowed.

'You aren't suggesting the two of us share that bedroom?' Andi frowned across the room at him, those chocolate-brown eyes gleaming with indignation.

Linus scowled darkly at Andi's obvious dismay at the mere suggestion they might have to share a bedroom for the night. What the hell did she think he was going to do, ravish her as soon as they were alone in the bedroom together?

Not that it was an altogether unacceptable idea when Andi was looking so damned beautiful; Linus just didn't like the obvious implication that he couldn't keep his hands—or any other part of his anatomy!—to himself.

His gaze narrowed. 'You would prefer that we go back out into the snow instead and try to look for somewhere that has two bedrooms available?'

'No, of course not.' She snapped her irritation. 'But—it—you could always sleep down here,' she added hopefully.

Apart from the armchair Linus was sitting in, there was only one other, and then bench seats and dining-room chairs placed about the empty tables.

He shook his head. 'I prefer the comfort of a bed. I have no objections to you sleeping down here if that's what you want to do,' he added harshly as Andi's frown deepened. 'Of course, the landlord might think that a little strange, as he seems to have assumed that we're a couple.'

'Then you can just *un*assume him!' The hand not holding the whisky glass clenched into a fist at Andi's side. 'I am not sharing a bedroom with you, Linus,' she repeated firmly.

'What is your problem, Andi?' Linus barked impatiently.

'I—you—we...' Andi gave an incredulous shake of her head, totally panicked—aware of him as she was—at the thought of sharing a bedroom with Linus. 'You're my boss. I work for you!'

His eyes glittered mockingly. 'And that precludes us sharing a bedroom?'

'According to you, yes!' she reminded him a little more desperately than she would have wished. 'You don't get involved with your female employees, remember?'

'Sharing a bedroom doesn't mean we're involved.'

'It doesn't mean we're *un*involved, either!'

Linus's gaze moved over her in slow appraisal. 'I'll keep my hands to myself if you will.'

'This is so—so ungentlemanly of you!'

Linus shrugged, unconcerned. 'I don't remember ever claiming to be a gentleman.'

'Just as well!' she breathed frustratedly. 'You—'

'We'll talk about this later, Andi,' Linus snapped, and turned questioningly to the landlord as he bustled back into the room.

'The missus already had some broth simmering in the pot,' the elderly man announced with satisfaction. 'She's put some bread in to bake to go with it while she goes upstairs to make the bed.'

It felt good to hear the faint Scottish burr in the other man's voice, making Linus realize how much he missed his homeland and the warmth of its people.

Linus had left Scotland years ago, of course, having accepted that he could either remain a big fish in a small pond or become an even bigger fish in a much bigger pond by moving to London and investing his money in property there. He had never regretted making that move—how could he when it had made him his fortune? But just hearing the Scottish accent again reminded him that this was still his home.

'How long do you expect this blizzard to last?' Andi was the one to question the landlord tightly.

'Och, this is no a blizzard,' the elderly man

assured her indulgently as he heard her English accent. 'This is no but a bit of a flurry.'

Andi's eyes widened. A bit of a flurry… God help them if it should turn into a blizzard!

'Sassenach,' Linus confided in the other man dryly.

Andi had absolutely no idea what that word meant, but she felt sure from the condescending smile that passed between the two men that it must be something derogatory. She gave Linus a censorious frown before turning back to the landlord. 'How long is this flurry expected to last, then?'

'No more than a couple of days,' he said dismissively.

'A couple of days?' Andi echoed with dismay as visions of herself and Linus marooned here for two days—and nights—popped unbidden into her head.

'A blizzard usually lasts a week or more.' The landlord nodded, unconcerned.

'How…reassuring,' Andi murmured weakly as she dropped down into the armchair opposite Linus's—a mockingly amused Linus if the taunting laughter in those pale, green eyes was anything to go by.

Andi could find nothing about this situation

that was in the least amusing. How could she, when just the thought of sharing a bedroom with Linus made her feel weak at the knees? Especially so after the intimacy of his earlier remarks.

'I'll just go and check on your food,' the landlord murmured nervously after shooting unhappy glances at Andi and Linus as their gazes remained locked in silent battle.

Andi sat forward in her chair once the two of them were alone. 'Linus, you really can't be serious about the two of us staying here and sharing a bedroom?'

Linus shrugged out of the warmth of his jacket before answering her. 'I'm open to any other suggestions you might have. Viable ones,' he added warningly as Andi would have spoken. He raised mocking brows as he settled back into his chair. 'Just because I'm a man and you're a woman does not mean I'm going to pounce on you as soon as we're alone in a bedroom together!'

Her cheeks flushed. 'I never imagined that it did.'

'Perhaps you think *you* might be tempted to pounce on me?'

Her eyes narrowed. 'Linus.'

'Andi?' he came back challengingly.

Once again Andi's chaotic thoughts were brought to an abrupt halt as instead she eyed Linus uncertainly, the dangerous glitter of his gaze enough to tell her she would be unwise to pursue this particular subject at the moment.

The whole idea of her and Linus sharing a bedroom for the night was unwise…

She drew in a ragged breath. 'This is all your fault.'

'I'm hardly responsible for the weather, Andi.' He gave an impatient shake of his head.

Her eyes darkened almost to black. 'You're responsible for my being in Scotland—that's enough reason for me to blame you entirely for this mess!'

'What mess?' he bit out impatiently. 'As the landlord has already said, this is nothing but a bit of a flurry. He shrugged. 'A couple of days and we can be on our way.'

'Just in time for your stupid rugby-match, I suppose? Twenty-two men trying to beat each other's heads in.'

'Thirty men—this is rugby, Andi, not football—and they aren't trying to "beat each other's heads in".' Linus's mouth tightened. 'The object of the game is to score tries by running with the ball and placing it over the line.'

'Whenever I've accidentally caught a glimpse of a match on television—as I'm changing channels, of course—'

'Oh, of course!'

She nodded. 'There just seems to be a tangle of arms, legs and bodies thrashing about on the ground.'

'That's because the other object of the game is for the opposing team to stop their opponents from scoring those tries.'

Andi gave a disdainful snort. 'I'm not convinced, Linus.'

'I'm not trying to convince you!' He stood up to pace impatiently. 'You're obviously a complete philistine when it comes to the magnificent game of rugby.'

'Magnificent!' She sniffed inelegantly. 'I suppose you know all about it?'

He gave a cool nod. 'As it happens, I do. I was record holder for the most tries and conversions scored my last year at school.'

'That explains a lot.'

Linus's gaze narrowed warningly. 'Would you care to explain?'

'No, I don't think I will.' Andi stood up in one fluid movement, relieved as she did so to find that her limbs had completely thawed out now. '"Sassenach"...?' she prompted scathingly.

Linus gave a dismissive shrug. 'Someone from England.'

Andi continued to look at him suspiciously for several seconds, sure there was more to that word than he was telling her; it had certainly sounded derogatory.

'I'm going to ask the landlord if he has a bathroom where I can freshen up,' she said abruptly. 'If you're serious about our staying here tonight.'

'Oh, I am, Andi,' he murmured huskily.

'Then our bags are still outside in the Range Rover,' she told him pointedly, her expression turning to one of quiet satisfaction as Linus's face creased into a pained grimace. He turned to look out of the window and realized he would have to go back out into the still heavily falling snow to retrieve those bags. 'Have fun!' Andi added tauntingly as she went through the doorway marked 'private'.

Her smile faded, however, as soon as she was alone in the hallway, and she paused to lean back weakly against the wall.

She couldn't share a bedroom with Linus

tonight. Possibly tomorrow night too, if the weather didn't let up. In fact, she trembled just at the thought of it.

Linus's complete dismissal of the significance of the two of them sharing a bedroom wasn't flattering, either.

Andi had been traumatized for months after her father and David had died. She hadn't so much as looked at another man, let alone been attracted to one. But slowly that insidious awareness of Linus had crept into her battered emotions. How could any healthy, red-blooded woman work with him on a day-to-day basis and not be aware of the hard vitality of his body and the rugged handsomeness of his chiselled features?

Andi certainly couldn't.

Which wasn't going to help the situation at all when Andi found herself alone in a bedroom with Linus later this evening!

CHAPTER THREE

'THERE'S only one bed!'

'And your point is…?' Linus came back dryly as he carried their bags into the small but comfortable bedroom that had been assigned to them for the night. A warming fire already burned in the small hearth; the only furniture in the room was a bed, a chair and a desk.

He had taken advantage of Andi's absence to pull his jacket back on and go back outside for their bags. The snow was still falling as heavily, and the wind just as remorseless and icy cold. Linus had been relieved just to make it back to the inn.

'You didn't say anything about there being only one bed,' Andi persisted, her cheeks flushed as she continued to stare at that bed.

Whether with temper or something else, Linus wasn't sure.

'Jim and Jennie have one daughter, hence

there's only one bed.' He dropped their bags onto the carpeted floor, completely ignoring Andi's pained wince as they landed with a thud.

Her gaze was accusing. 'You *knew* there was only one bed?'

Linus shrugged. 'I guessed that might be the case, yes. Stop being such a damned prude, Andi.' He scowled as she continued to look at him wide-eyed.

The heated emotions Linus aroused in Andi were totally new to her, and all the more disturbing. Because, although Andi had been engaged to marry David, she had never been so completely physically aware of him as she was Linus. She was so aware of him that she trembled just at the thought of having to share that bed with him.

If Andi had learnt anything about Linus the last year, it was that he had absolutely no interest in a permanent relationship. That the moment any of the women who flitted in and out of his bed on a regular basis showed any signs of expecting a commitment from him, they were quietly and discreetly excluded from his life.

Linus had informed her only yesterday that such exclusion had also included any of his previous PAs who had shown an interest in a personal relationship with him.

'Maybe you're worried, sharing a bed, *you* might be driven mad with lust for *me*?' Linus mocked softly.

'Hardly,' Andi snapped.

'Then there's no problem, is there?' He dismissed her unconcerned.

Andi drew in a sharp breath. 'Have you shared a bed with any woman in the last twenty years or so and not made love with her?'

'Of course I—' Linus broke off his instant rebuttal to give the question careful consideration instead. 'No, I never have,' he finally conceded. 'But I'm sure there has to be a first time for everything.'

'Does there?'

'You know, you're really starting to irritate me now, Andi,' he rasped harshly. 'Okay, so you're beautiful and you have a fantastic body—especially in those tight denims and that body-hugging green sweater you're currently wearing—but that doesn't mean I'm going to attempt to make love to you the moment I have you alone in a bed!'

Andi's thoughts were in turmoil. Linus thought she was beautiful and had a fantastic body…

The knowledge almost made her want to groan out loud. It certainly made her completely aware of the tight denims and body-hugging green sweater she was currently wearing.

'Well, that's really helped to clarify the situation,' she muttered disgustedly. 'I'll sleep in the chair.'

Linus arched dark brows. 'Trying to make me feel bad, Andi?'

'Am I succeeding?'

'No.' He grimaced.

'That's what I thought.' She gave a rueful nod.

Andi looked at him searchingly, noting as she did so the lines of tiredness beside his eyes and mouth. Those sculptured lips that had surely been designed to drive a woman wild…

Stop it, Andi, she instantly instructed herself firmly. Imagining what it would be like to be kissed by Linus, to feel his lips and hands on her body, really wasn't helping this already fraught situation.

Why was it that just looking at Linus made her so physically aware of both herself and him?

She sighed. 'It would have been much simpler if you had just corrected the landlord when he assumed we were a couple.'

Linus shrugged, unconcerned. 'Even if I had explained our working relationship to the landlord I still doubt it would have made a difference. There is only one room. Besides, you're a beautiful woman, Andi, and I'm a red-blooded man,' he explained impatiently. Andi's frown did not detract in the slightest from that ethereal beauty.

Her hair had dried now, falling in silky waves onto her shoulders, those brown eyes dark and unfathomable; the colour had returned to her cheeks, and her lips were full and inviting above her stubbornly pointed chin.

Andi was beautiful. Incredibly so. So why had their relationship remained on a platonic level this last year?

Because Linus knew now that Andi really *was* the best PA in the western hemisphere, and a shift in that relationship to the physical would definitely put their working relationship under considerable strain, if it didn't end it completely.

Besides which, Andi was obviously still in mourning for that vile Simmington-Browne.

Several times in the last year Linus had been tempted to shatter her rosy-hued illusions about her deceased fiancé. But each time he had resisted the temptation. There was no guarantee that Andi would believe him, anyway; she seemed to have put Simmington-Browne on some sort of pedestal this last year, to the point that there had been no other men in her life since the other man had died.

Fortunately, Simmington-Browne's secrets had died with him. It was a knowledge that Linus, when he'd learnt the truth only months after the other man's death, had chosen to keep to himself too. And he would continue to keep it to himself.

Unless Andi pushed him into doing otherwise…

'You still should have tried to explain our real relationship,' Andi insisted stubbornly. 'But obviously it's too late now.' She grimaced.

'Obviously,' Linus drawled dismissively.

Her gaze was frosty. 'I suggest we both return downstairs. Our food is probably ready by now.'

'I'll join you in a few minutes,' Linus replied wearily. 'Like you, I need to freshen up before we eat,' he added tersely as Andi paused to give him a searching look. 'I take it we're also sharing a bathroom with the landlord and his wife?'

'It would appear so,' Andi nodded. The bathroom she had used earlier was a short distance down the hallway, and contained toiletries for both men and women. 'It's very kind of them to offer us the use of their daughter's bedroom in this way.'

Linus nodded. 'I suggest you tell them that when you get downstairs.'

'I intended doing so,' she snapped, her eyes glittering with resentment at Linus's rebuke. 'It's you I'm annoyed with, Linus, not Jim and his wife.'

'Lucky, lucky me,' he drawled dryly.

'You're impossible!' Andi told him impatiently.

He shrugged unrepentantly. 'So I'm told.'

Then Andi remembered. She had his Aunt Mae to meet in the next few days. Surely she wasn't expecting Andi and Linus to share a bedroom too...?

'I trust that your Aunt Mae, at least, is aware of our separate sleeping arrangements?' Andi prompted tartly.

'Perfectly.' Linus's gaze silently laughed at her. 'In fact, I think you might come as something of a surprise to my Aunt Mae.'

Andi eyed him warily. 'In what way?'

He shrugged dismissive shoulders. 'I believe she may have the impression that you are slightly older than you actually are.'

Andi's frown deepened. 'And why would she think that?'

Linus raised dark brows. 'Probably because the description "prim, officious and efficient" sounds like it belongs to an older woman.'

Andi's eyes widened. 'Is that what you told your aunt about me?'

'You don't think the description fits?'

Well, yes, it fitted. It just sounded so *boring*, Andi acknowledged unhappily. Dry and boring—desiccated, even. She sounded like a woman twice her age!

Was that really how Linus saw her? If he did, then Andi obviously needed to have absolutely no worries concerning sharing a bedroom with him tonight.

'Wonderful,' she muttered resentfully. 'Perhaps you should ring her and tell her that we've been delayed?'

'That's very thoughtful of you, Andi, but I called her before bringing up the bags,' Linus replied dismissively. 'The snow is as bad in Ayr, so she had already guessed we might have to stop off somewhere along the way.'

Only Andi, it seemed, was dissatisfied with their current sleeping-arrangements.

Although she cheered up slightly when the 'broth' turned out to be a huge bowl of meaty stew, accompanied by freshly baked bread and soft, golden butter. The four of them ate together in the small dining-room off the main bar. The landlord's wife Jennie was a plump, middle-aged woman whose warmth at the two unexpected guests thrust upon her was nevertheless completely genuine.

'We Scots are a warm and friendly lot once you get past the outer dourness,' Linus answered dryly at Andi's comment to that effect once Jim and Jennie had retired to the kitchen, after refusing their offer to help tidy away the remains of the meal.

Andi had never really thought of Linus as being Scottish—although, with a name like Linus Harrison, he could hardly be anything else! But she had noticed a slight burr returning to his normally well-modulated voice as he'd conversed with the older couple during the meal, an accent he had obviously deliberately erased during the years he had spent in England.

It was mortifying for Andi to realize how totally aware of Linus she had become in the last few months, and especially in the last few hours, that she now found even that slight lilt in his voice attractive.

'Then obviously I've never got past yours!' she came back tartly to hide her inner turmoil.

His lids lowered slightly over pale, green eyes as he studied her. 'Did you want to?'

Andi felt her cheeks warm under that penetrating gaze. 'Of course not,' she snapped. 'I'm employed as your PA, Linus. Consequently, your demeanour, dour or otherwise, is of no relevance to me.'

His brows rose. 'I thought I heard a slight edge of censure in your voice.'

'You didn't.'

'Oh yes, Andi.' Linus reached across the table to cover her hand with one of his as he gazed deeply into her eyes. 'I most certainly did.'

Andi couldn't look away, but instead found herself mesmerized by those amazing eyes. 'This isn't a good idea, Linus...' Her words came out as a breathless sigh.

No, it wasn't, Linus conceded. But for the moment, looking into those melting eyes, caressing Andi's fingers with his own, Linus couldn't think of anything else.

'Linus?'

The slightly panicked edge to her voice penetrated Linus's concentration on her slightly parted, eminently kissable lips.

Andi had worked for him for a year now, the two of them often working closely together on

the alterations to Tarrington Hall. While Linus
might subconsciously always have been aware
of her as a beautiful woman, he had never
wanted to cross the employer-employee boundary. Until now.

Something had happened in the last few
hours to change that. But what?

He had never touched her before, Linus
realized slightly dazed. He had never held Andi
in his arms the way he'd done as he'd battled his
way through the snow to the inn. Had never experienced the way she'd clung to him still even
once they'd been inside the inn. Had never
touched her hand in the way he was doing now,
been able to feel the silky softness of her skin
against his own.

'You're right,' he rasped, releasing her hand
to sit back.

Andi's fingers tingled from the touch of
Linus's, her cheeks feeling flushed, her eyes
feverish. Just because Linus had touched her?
Oh God…

Had she been alone so long, been so totally,
absolutely self-contained, that just the touch
of a man's hand—the touch of Linus's
hand—had reawakened all her senses, both
tactile and visual? Because just looking at

Linus now told her how aware she was of everything about him.

His long, dark hair was slightly tousled, and a temptation for any woman to run her fingers through its silky softness. His eyes, those pale, all-seeing green eyes, were shuttered now, hiding his thoughts from other probing eyes. His face looked as if it had been hewn out of rock, perfect in its rugged handsomeness. His shoulders were wide and muscled beneath his thick, black sweater, his stomach taut and flat, his hips lean, and his legs long in the faded black denims.

Linus Harrison, Andi acknowledged with dismay, was the most sexily attractive man she had ever set eyes on.

Except she hadn't really seen him the last year, as she'd continued to grieve for David and her father. Well, most of that year... In the last six months she had begun to see and recognize Linus as a dangerously attractive man. She had just known it was better to keep that realization buried beneath her usual cool demeanour. Beneath her 'prim, officious and efficient' demeanour!

God, how that description rankled. Enough for her to want to prove otherwise? No, it certainly didn't rankle that much.

She stood up abruptly. 'I think I'll go up to bed.'

Linus looked up at her with lazily amused eyes. 'I thought you had decided to sleep in the chair?'

Andi shot him an irritated frown. 'If you insist on sleeping in the bed, yes!'

'Oh, I insist.' He nodded unrelentingly, before sighing as he saw her pained expression. 'It doesn't have to be this way, Andi.'

'It most certainly does.'

'Oh, for goodness' sake, Andi, you can always put a wall of pillows down the middle of the bed if that makes you feel safer!' he snapped impatiently.

Nothing about sharing a bedroom with Linus made Andi feel safe. And that uncertainty had nothing to do with Linus's intentions towards her and everything to do with her own confused emotions. 'I'm merely trying to be sensible, Linus.'

'You're merely behaving like some Victorian virgin who fears for her innocence,' he came back cuttingly.

Maybe because that was exactly what she was. Oh, not the Victorian part, but a virgin certainly. Andi could easily understand how that would seem an impossibility to Linus, when she was almost twenty-eight years old and had been engaged to be married just over a year ago. But when she'd been at university Andi hadn't wanted to enter into the same casual relationships her friends had. And David's whirlwind courtship of her had been new when he'd died so unexpectedly, and they hadn't given any thought to going to bed together, had never progressed beyond sharing a few passionate kisses.

So here she was—Andrea Buttonfield—an almost-twenty-eight-year-old virgin.

'Don't be ridiculous, Linus,' she snapped. 'I am merely trying to maintain the formality of our working relationship.'

His mouth twisted humourlessly. 'Perhaps if I were to give you some dictation before we fall asleep?'

'I don't take dictation—of any kind,' Andi assured him waspishly.

'No, you don't, do you?' Linus conceded wearily. 'Okay, Andi, you win; I'll sleep in the chair. I hope that isn't a smile of triumph I see on your lips,' he added slowly, his gaze narrowing.

'Of course not,' she assured him, her expression innocent.

Too innocent, Linus acknowledged impatiently. 'As I have to suffer the discomfort of sleeping in the chair, I think I'll stay down here and enjoy another glass of whisky before coming upstairs.' It would also give Andi the time and privacy she needed to get into bed.

In truth, Linus wasn't any more comfortable now with the idea of sharing a bedroom with Andi either; those few minutes of awareness a short time ago told him that they weren't as immune to each other as he would have wished.

Her skin had felt as soft as velvet, and just as sensuous; the laughter in her eyes a few seconds ago had been warm and inviting. The promise of gently swaying hips as she left the room to go upstairs was an enticement Linus wasn't sure he could resist once alone in a bedroom with her.

What the hell was *wrong* with him? It wasn't as if he was feeling sexually deprived. Admittedly, his most recent relationship had come to an end several months ago, but that certainly didn't explain his sudden awareness of Andi and his heated thoughts about her. The cool, the distant, the stylish Andrea Buttonfield.

Except she no longer seemed as cool, or quite so distant…

CHAPTER FOUR

'WILL you please stop fidgeting and just go to sleep?'

Andi instantly became still in the bed. 'I can't seem to get comfortable.' Linus's presence in the room had Andi on edge.

'Then maybe I got the better part of the deal after all,' Linus murmured with satisfaction. 'This chair isn't half bad.'

'Sadist!'

He laughed softly in the darkness. The only light in the room came from the damped down fire and the moonlight reflecting the pristine-white snow outside as it shone through the window. 'Do you want to swap?' he offered irritably as Andi began to fidget again.

'Then you wouldn't be comfortable.'

'It wasn't my impression earlier that you cared about my comfort.' Linus lay on his back, staring up at the ceiling. He did his damnedest to block out the memory of Andi snuggled under the bedclothes when he'd come up to the room, her golden hair cascading across the pillow beneath her, her eyes dark and luminous as she'd looked across at him.

'I gave you one of the blankets.' Her tone was slightly indignant.

'One of them,' he conceded dryly. 'It may have escaped your notice, Andi, snuggled up cosily beneath the bedclothes as you are, but it's damned cold in here in spite of the fire.'

Andi sat up to punch her pillows into a more comfortable shape, inwardly aware that it wasn't the bed that was uncomfortable but her. She was just so aware of Linus as he lounged in the chair a short distance away. She could hear the even tenor of his breathing. Could just feel his presence mere feet away.

And she didn't want to be aware of any of those things.

'Andi, will you just go to sleep?'

'You aren't asleep either, despite claiming earlier that you were exhausted.'

'If you don't settle down and go to sleep soon, then I'm going to come over there and join you!'

Andi became very still, barely breathing, but at the same time was aware of the rapid beat of her heart. So loud that surely Linus must be able to hear it.

'I thought that might quieten you down.' Linus chuckled softly in the darkness.

She lay still, willing herself not to move, not to show by so much as a twitch that she was completely aware of Linus and the promise behind his words.

What was wrong with her? Linus was her boss, and had been for the last year. Admittedly, they had never been away on business together before, let alone had to share a bedroom, but even so she wasn't handling this very well.

Andi was also aware that she was the one occupying the bed while Linus tried to make himself comfortable in the armchair. That he was the employer and she was the employee.

She drew in a ragged breath, wanting desperately to invite Linus to share the bed, but fearing what might happen.

Andi squeaked in panic as she suddenly became aware of Linus getting up to cross the room before standing ominously beside the bed.

'I've had enough of this,' he conceded as he moved to lie on the bed beside her.

She stared up at him with wide, apprehensive eyes. 'Linus...'

'I've decided to just get this out of the way and then maybe we can both get some sleep!' he rasped purposefully.

'This' being to lower his head before his mouth claimed Andi's in a kiss that totally robbed her of breath. Of resistance.

Resistance? As soon as Linus's lips found hers, parting them to deepen the kiss, his arms moulding her body close to his despite the bedclothes that separated them, Andi completely melted, both physically and emotionally.

He tasted so good; his lips felt so sure and purposeful against hers, his body hard and muscled as he half-lay across her, his weight exquisite as he pressed her down into the mattress and his hands roamed restlessly down the length of her body.

Andi freed her arms, gasping slightly as her hands came into contact with the heated bareness of his shoulders and then lingered there. Linus felt so warm and strong beneath her fingers, muscles rippling. She couldn't control her hands as they moved caressingly over that firmness, before exploring the curved planes of his back and down to his waist, and then lower still to caress the tense hardness of his bare buttocks.

Dear God, Linus was completely naked!

Andi began to struggle, her hands moving to push against his chest even as she wrenched her mouth away from his. 'What are you doing?' she gasped breathlessly.

That was far better than he had anticipated, and sleep was now the last thing on his mind!

He moved back slightly to look down at Andi, easily able to discern the angry, dark glitter of her eyes. 'I don't know about you, but I'm unlikely to get any sleep at all now!' he acknowledged. 'Unless, of course, you feel in the mood to finish what we just started…?' he prompted.

'No, I do not feel in the mood to finish what *you* just started!' Andi snapped indignantly. And once again she pushed against his chest.

'For your information, I was not expecting you to make a pass, as you call it. She scooted to the side of the bed, as far away from him as it was possible to be without actually getting out of it. 'Have I ever given you reason to believe I wanted you to kiss me?'

He tilted his head, considering. 'Until just now, you mean?'

Andi's eyes had adjusted enough now in the dimness of the reflected light in the room to be able to see Linus in all his naked glory; he looked as good as she had imagined he would. His shoulders and chest were wide and powerful, his waist tapered, his thighs... He was aroused!

Her gaze quickly returned to the hard planes of Linus's face. 'Not even then,' she challenged firmly. '*You* kissed *me*.'

'You kissed me right back,' he challenged.

Andi drew in a hissing breath, the fact that she knew she deserved the accusation only increasing her anger. 'You were all over me before I had a chance to protest.'

'You were all over me too,' he rasped. 'All the way from my shoulders down to my—'

'I didn't know you were naked!' she defended herself.

He shrugged unconcerned shoulders. 'So now you know.'

Andi glared at him frustratedly. 'Will you just get off the bed and go back to the chair?'

His mouth tightened. 'No, I don't think that I will.'

'No?' Andi stared at him incredulously.

'Lower your voice, will you?' Linus hissed. 'Jim and Jennie will think we're having an argument.'

'We *are* having an argument!'

'No, Andi, *you're* having an argument,' Linus taunted her. 'I just want to get some sleep.' He moved slightly so that he could slip beneath the bedclothes. 'That feels good,' he murmured as he settled comfortably on the pillows, placing his hands behind his head.

Andi sat up to stare at him. 'You can't sleep there!'

'I hate to contradict you, Andi, but this is exactly where I intend sleeping.' He yawned as if to prove the point.

'No you are not!'

'Who's going to stop me?' He opened one derisive eye as he turned to look at her.

Andi was infuriated, enraged by his mocking attitude. That wasn't the only thing infuriating her, she acknowledged in self-disgust, but for the moment that was what she intended to focus on.

'You're despicable!' she snapped as she climbed out of the other side of the bed. 'I can't believe that you intend making me sleep in the chair!' She stood beside the bed, glaring down at him as he lay comfortably beneath the warm covers, repressing her own shiver at how cold it had become in the bedroom now that the fire had died down slightly.

Linus shrugged. 'You're the one who's insisting on sleeping in the chair.'

'Only because you aren't gentlemanly enough to—'

'That's the second time you've made that accusation!' Linus got out of the bed and stood up so fast that Andi didn't have time to move away, her arms now grasped tightly in his steely fingers as he looked down at her with angrily gleaming eyes. 'I suppose Simmington-Browne would have slept in the chair without argument?' he taunted.

'David was certainly a gentleman—' She broke off abruptly as that gleam in Linus's eyes turned to a dangerous glitter. 'Obviously it would have been different if I was here with David,' she said stiffly.

Linus's mouth twisted. 'You mean you wouldn't have felt the same reluctance at sleeping with him?'

Andi stiffened. 'I don't believe it was sleep you had in mind a few minutes ago.'

'You're right, it wasn't,' Linus teased.

He didn't have sleep in mind now, either. He might have his arousal under control but it was definitely still there. Looking at Andi as she stood so ethereal and lovely in her pale nightgown wasn't helping that situation—although talking of Simmington-Browne was certainly putting a damper on the proceedings.

Andi seemed to have built up such a memory of her fiancé in the last year or so that to her he now appeared to be some sort of untarnished god. Linus had absolutely no doubts that in Andi's eyes *he* didn't measure up to that glowing image. Or anyone else, judging by the fact that Andi didn't seem to have had so much as a single date the last year.

'Take the bed,' he rasped. 'I believe I'll settle for the chair after all.'

She looked at Linus suspiciously for several long seconds. 'What guarantee do I have that you aren't going to change your mind halfway through the night?'

'Andi, what have I ever said or done to give you the impression I find you so irresistible?' There was a steely edge to his voice.

Andi felt the colour drain from her cheeks. 'I wasn't implying you found me irresistible.'

'The alternative, then, seems to be that you believe me incapable of sharing a bedroom, let alone a bed, with any woman without attempting to make love to her.'

'I suggest we just forget this, and the conversation, and get some sleep,' she muttered wearily as she climbed back into the bed. 'I'm sure that everything will look different in the morning.' She was also hoping that by morning the snow would have melted away completely and they could continue with their journey.

Although she very much doubted that that would be the case…

It wasn't.

Andi didn't even need to climb out of the warmth of the bed to know that the snow was still on the ground. She could tell from the brightness of the daylight filtering into the room between the undrawn curtains that the reason for that brightness was the light reflecting on the snow outside. All sound seemed slightly muffled by that soft whiteness.

She hadn't slept well. She couldn't stop thinking. How could she after Linus had kissed her, when she had kissed him back? When she was so totally aware of him across the room as he once again made himself comfortable in the armchair?

Andi had lain awake for what seemed like hours after she'd been sure Linus had fallen asleep, unable to put the memory of that kiss out of her mind. Or the fact that she had responded. More than responded; she had wanted more. Much more. Her body was still aching and restless from the desire Linus had ignited with that single kiss, and from the guilt she was slowly feeling for her late fiancé.

She must have dozed off some time during the night, although the aching lethargy of her body told her that it had not been a refreshing sleep.

Only Andi's eyes moved as she checked on whether Linus was still in the bedroom with her.

He lay sprawled in the armchair, that single blanket wrapped around his torso and thighs, thank goodness, leaving the long length of his legs and feet bared.

He really was a magnificent specimen of virile manhood. Who was she kidding? Linus was absolutely gorgeous! That slightly over-long dark hair was tousled now and falling endearingly over his forehead. The hardness of his features was relaxed in sleep, making him appear much younger than his thirty-six years.

Andi admired the masculine perfection of Linus's body: shoulders broad, arms muscled, chest and stomach flat, thighs powerful; his bare legs were long and still tanned from the holiday he had taken in the Bahamas over the

Christmas period. Even his feet were attractive, so long and slender.

What was wrong with her?

Her engagement to David, having been followed weeks later by his untimely death, contributed to make Andi shy away from becoming involved with men. Least of all with a man like Linus, who never made any effort to hide his complete allergy to long-term relationships.

Worse, she was Linus's PA, and he had made it more than clear that he never, ever became involved with the women who worked for him—that they would no longer continue to work for him if that became the case. Would Linus class last night's kiss as 'involvement'?

More to the point, did Andi class that kiss as involvement?

Linus felt cramped, unrested and decidedly bad-tempered when he woke up. The fact that Andi had got up some time during the night to cover him with a second blanket did very little to lighten his mood.

So it was as well that Andi had already left the bedroom, probably in search of breakfast. Or possibly a way out of here! Linus very much doubted that she would relish the idea of staying on, sharing this bedroom with him, for a second night.

One glance out of the window showed Linus that she was out of luck. Yet more snow seemed to have fallen during the night. At least nine or ten inches of it covered the ground around the Range Rover, with drifts two or three feet deep in places.

Linus glanced back at the empty bed. The fact that it was now neatly remade did not detract from his memories of lying there with Andi the previous night. Of kissing her. Touching her.

She had the sexiest mouth he had ever kissed, so soft and yielding, her lips full and sensual. As for that curvaceous body…

Linus gave a low groan as his body stirred just thinking about how good Andi had felt when he'd pulled her close against him, her curves full and luscious to the touch.

If he intended her to continue working for him, then he should stop these thoughts right now!

Andi eyed Linus warily as he came into the large kitchen where she lingered over her second cup of coffee. The single slice of toast she had eaten for her breakfast seemed to have settled the butterflies in her stomach.

Or, at least, it had until she was once again
face to face with Linus. Jennie, the landlady,
had excused herself a few minutes ago to go and
light the fire in the bar while Jim cleared the
snow from the front doorway. It didn't help that
Linus was looking particularly ruggedly attractive in an Aran sweater and black denims.

'Coffee?' she offered Linus briskly.

'Thanks.' He nodded before moving to sit in
the chair opposite hers at the table.

Andi got up to get another mug and bring the
pot of steaming coffee to the table. 'Milk and
sugar?' She kept her tone deliberately light as
she poured the coffee.

Linus gave her a scowling glance. 'In the year
you've worked for me have I ever taken either?'

'Well…no.' Andi felt the warmth of colour
entering her cheeks. 'I was just being polite,
Linus,' she added, exasperated as he remained
unimpressed.

So it was going to be like that, was it? Linus
accepted it as he took a welcome sip of his black,
unsweetened coffee before leaning back in his
chair to look across at Andi with narrowed, as-
sessing eyes. The no-nonsense style of her hair,
secured in a band at her nape, should have told
him how things stood between them today.

'Is politeness to be the order of the day?' he taunted.

Andi stiffened as she heard his obvious mockery. 'I trust that I am always polite, Linus.'

'You weren't very polite last night,' Linus challenged.

He raised dark brows. 'And, as I remember, you implied that I lack the attributes of a gentleman.'

Andi shook her head, her efforts at politeness obviously completely wasted when Linus was in this provoking mood. 'I didn't imply it at all, Linus!'

Linus's eyes narrowed to pale-green slits. 'You also implied Simmington-Browne would have behaved differently in the same circumstances.' His voice was deceptively soft.

Nevertheless Andi heard that slight edge of contempt that crept into Linus's tone whenever David entered their conversation. 'Did you and David ever meet?' she prompted, wondering what the sophisticated and cultured David would have made of the ruggedly forceful, self-made millionaire Linus Harrison.

'That doesn't answer my question, Andi.'

'You haven't answered mine either.'

Linus's mouth twisted humourlessly. 'I'll

answer yours if you'll answer mine,' he came back, taunting.

'David, I am sure, would have slept in the chair without complaint. In fact, I doubt he would have insisted on sharing the bedroom with me at all. He would probably have offered to sleep downstairs in one of the chairs in the bar,' she added.

'He hardly sounds like a man!' Linus muttered disgustedly.

Andi bristled resentfully. 'How dare you—?'

'I'm merely commenting on the lack of red blood in the man's veins.' Linus shrugged dismissively.

'You were insulting a man who isn't here to defend himself.' She glared at him.

There were several things Linus would have liked to say to David Simmington-Browne if he had him alone in a room right now. Not least that the man hadn't deserved to have a woman as sexy and as loyal as Andrea Buttonfield fall in love with him.

'I find your attitude distasteful.'

'I'm beginning to think you find everything about me distasteful!' Linus rasped as he stood up. 'Which makes me wonder why you came to work for me in the first place.'

'As I recall, you didn't give me much choice in the matter!' Andi's cheeks were very pale, her eyes huge, brown wells of emotion in that pallor.

A nerve pulsed in Linus's tightly clenched jaw. 'Would you like me to give you the choice now?'

Andi frowned, knowing—as no doubt Linus did too—she didn't really have that choice. Not only did she need and like this job as Linus's PA, but keeping it also ensured that her mother could continue to live at the gate house. 'I don't think this is the appropriate time to discuss this, Linus.'

'Perhaps you'll let me know when you think it is the appropriate time,' Linus bit out before turning sharply on his heel and striding forcefully across the room.

Andi watched him dazedly. 'Where are you going?'

His eyes blazed as he glanced back at her. 'To help Jim clear some of the snow away, of course. With any luck, we'll be able to dig ourselves out of here some time later today!' The door closed forcefully behind him.

Andi breathed shakily as she slumped back in her chair, totally bewildered by their conversation. By the anger boiling beneath the surface in both of them.

Andi knew the reason for her own anger. It

was not towards Linus, but towards herself—for dropping her guard so badly last night that she could see no way back to their previous relationship of employer and employee.

The reason for Linus's anger, however, was a complete mystery to her. Except she knew that it was there. Forceful. Harsh.

Dangerous…

CHAPTER FIVE

'GET your coat on, Andi. We're going for a walk,' Linus encouraged her abruptly once lunch was over and Andi sat huddled beside the warm fire in the bar.

She didn't look impressed by his suggestion as she turned to glance out of the frosted window. 'It's been snowing again.'

'I noticed,' Linus drawled. The snow had started to fall again as he'd helped Jim spade the worst of it away from the pathway leading to the front of the inn. 'Come on, Andi,' he cajoled. 'It will be fun!'

She grimaced. 'I can't see any fun in getting cold and wet.'

Linus eyed her darkly. Was she still annoyed with him over their conversation earlier this morning? 'Didn't you ever go out and play in the snow when you were a child?'

She raised blonde brows. 'On the rare occasions that it snowed in Hampshire, my father always insisted we go to a warmer clime.'

'What about after you moved to London?'

'It rarely snowed when I lived in London.'

'And no doubt when it did you stayed huddled indoors until it had completely melted away?' he guessed.

'Of course.'

'Haven't you ever been skiing?'

'Well, of course I've been skiing.' Andi gave him a disdainful glance. 'Every winter when I was young, and several times since. But skiing is something else entirely.'

Linus gave a disbelieving shake of his head. 'You've never walked in the snow just for the hell of it?'

'Certainly not.' Andi frowned.

'Unbelievable.' Linus grimaced. And he had always thought his childhood had been deprived! At least his mother, and latterly Aunt Mae, had allowed him to enjoy being a boy. 'All the more reason for us to go out in the snow now, then,' he prompted. 'Come on, Andi; I'll teach you how to make and throw snowballs.'

She eyed him unenthusiastically. 'I've already told you, I have no desire to end up wet and cold.'

She was still annoyed with him. 'That's half the fun.'

'Maybe to you it is,' she came back. 'Linus, I'm perfectly happy where I am, thank you very much. What are you doing?' she protested as Linus crossed the room in two long strides to take hold of her arm and pull her effortlessly to her feet. 'I am not going outside, Linus!' Her eyes sparkled rebelliously as he began to march her towards the door.

He came to an abrupt halt, green gaze narrowing as he looked down at her. 'The way I see it, Andi, you have two choices. You can either put on your coat, hat and gloves, and come outside with me willingly. Or—' he paused for effect '—I'm going to just pick you up exactly as you are before I carry you outside and drop you into a snowdrift!'

Andi stared up at Linus, her earlier anger now added to by indignation as he refused to let her shake off the tightness of his grip on her arm. 'I don't want—'

'Too late; you had your chance.' Linus bent and swung her up effortlessly into his arms before striding towards the door.

'Linus, stop this!' Andi squirmed frantically in his arms. 'Linus, put me down!' she ordered furiously as she pushed ineffectually against the hardness of his chest.

'Nope.' His face teased her. 'Snowdrift, here you come,' he warned as he bent slightly to open the door, at once admitting a cold blast of wind and snow.

'These are expensive boots! If you ruin them—'

'I'll replace them,' Linus came back mildly, having paused in the open doorway. 'Make your mind up, Andi. Willingly, or not?' He gave a devilish grin as he eyed one of the deep snow-drifts outside.

'Okay, okay!' Andi cried protestingly, glaring up at him, knowing he would make good on his threat if she didn't comply. 'I'll go and change these boots and get my coat,' she muttered impatiently. 'But the first thing I'm going to do when I get outside is stuff a nice, big, wet snowball down your neck!' she warned as Linus slowly placed her back on her feet.

He grinned down at her, unconcerned. 'You'll have to catch me first.'

'Don't worry,' she grated. 'I'll catch you!'

'Now you're getting into the spirit of it.'

'No—now I'm going to take my revenge!' she assured him.

He was nothing but a bully, Andi decided as she stomped up the stairs to collect her hat and coat. A heartless, uncaring bully. A sexy, heartless, uncaring bully. A very sexy bully...

Andi sank down onto the side of the bed. The bed where Linus had lain with her, so briefly, the night before.

Damn it, she was never going to be able to think of him as just Linus Harrison, her employer, ever again.

When Andi had first started working with Linus she had been annoyed at the way he had manoeuvred her into it, and because of that she had been determined not to be impressed by him.

But over the following weeks and months it had been impossible not to admire the astuteness of his mind. To acknowledge his unerring ability to look at something and see its possibilities from a business angle. To see how he knew instinctively how something could be improved and honed so that it became beautiful as well as financially viable.

When, exactly, had that appreciation of Linus's business acumen turned into something much more personal on Andi's side? When had that admiration for Linus's business acumen turned to a personal attraction?

Andi had still been deeply traumatized by David and her father's deaths when she'd begun working for Linus, but as that numbness had begun to fade she had found herself becoming aware of him as more than just her boss. She would find herself looking at him, studying him, when she hadn't even been aware of doing so.

She'd realized how those ruggedly hewn features could make her heart beat a little faster. How his eyes could be so cold and compelling one minute and then wickedly sensual the next. Most of all she'd found herself looking at his mouth; his bottom lip was slightly fuller than the top one; his teeth were very white and even when he gave one of his wolfish grins, or less often a burst of full-throated laughter. And his hands... Linus had long hands that he moved with unconscious grace, the fingers slender, the nails kept short.

Andi had found herself wondering how it would feel to have those hands caressing her. Or how his mouth would feel against hers if he should ever kiss her. Soft and sensual? Or hard and demanding?

After last night she had the answer to those two questions at least, Andi reminded herself as she stood up impatiently. The answer was both, of course. Hard and demanding initially, and then becoming soft and sensually enticing when she'd responded.

Forget it, Andi, she told herself firmly as she picked up her coat and gloves. Linus was her boss. If Andi wanted him to remain that way, to also ensure that her mother could continue to live in the gate house at Tarrington Park, then she had damn well better forget last night had ever happened.

'You aren't still mad at me?' Linus prompted as Andi walked silently beside him in the snow in the direction of the pine forest at the back of the inn. The majestic trees were weighted down by the snowfall.

Andi had been upstairs much longer than Linus had expected, and he had been on the verge of climbing the stairs to go and get her. But before he could do so Andi had arrived back downstairs in the bar, having changed her expensive boots for walking boots that she had tartly informed him she had brought with her to wear to the match on Sunday. She was also wearing her coat and gloves, with a woollen hat pulled on over her hair and dark glasses perched on the bridge of her nose against the glare of the snow, effectively shielding the expression in her eyes from his searching gaze.

'I wasn't aware that I was mad at you.' She shrugged, her face red and glowing, her breath a delicate mist in the coldness of the air.

Before Linus was even aware of what she was doing, Andi had bent down, scooped up some snow and successfully dropped the icy coldness down the front of his sweater, taking advantage of the fact that his gloveless hands were pushed into the pockets of his coat.

'Why, you little—!' Linus finally managed to free his hands to scoop up some snow of his own, pelting her with it before bending down to scoop up some more and throw that at her too.

What followed was a free-for-all of badly aimed snowballs on Andi's part and more accurate ones on Linus's. Both of them ended up splattered with damp snow and out of breath ten minutes or so later.

'Truce!' Linus raised freezing-cold hands, grinning broadly. 'I can't feel my fingers, they're so cold!'

'Serves you right,' Andi came back unsympathetically, her grin as wide as his.

'Admit it, Andi, it was fun.'

'It was fun,' she acknowledged ruefully. 'Especially as you now look like the Abominable Snowman!' She chuckled lightly as she looked at Linus, his hair in wet tendrils about his face, his coat and black denims covered in snow.

He looked about him admiringly as by tacit consent they turned to resume their walk towards the forest. 'I'd forgotten how clear the air is up here. How unspoilt it all is.'

'Do you miss it?' Andi prompted.

Linus shrugged. 'Sometimes. Other times I remember how frustrated I felt when I was younger and playing on the streets in Glasgow, and then how little there was for me to do as a teenager living with my aunt in a little hamlet outside Ayr.'

Andi eyed him quizzically. Linus had never talked to her of his early life before. 'You moved to live with her after your mother died, didn't you?' That much Andi had learnt from the occasional newspaper article on him.

His smile faded. 'Yes.'

'Not your father?'

'No,' he bit out. 'I never knew my father. Or, to put it more accurately, he never knew me.' He grimaced.

She shook her head. 'I don't understand.'

Linus's smile had a slightly bitter edge. 'About ten years ago I made it my business to meet him.'

'And?'

'And nothing,' he stated flatly. 'Oh, I could see the similarities between us. The colouring; my mother and Aunt Mae are—were— redheads,' he added affectionately. 'The build, maybe.' He shrugged. 'I saw the similarities between us, but when I looked at him I felt nothing.' He frowned slightly. 'Absolutely nothing,' he repeated.

'Did you expect to?' Andi asked gently.

Linus turned to look at her, his smile ironic. 'Strangely enough, I did. All those years of growing up without a father had made me curious as to what sort of man he was. Oh, I knew from my mother that she had met him while living in London. That he was a lawyer, an ambitious lawyer, who didn't want a wife and baby in his life at that time to tie him down,' he grated harshly. 'My mother kept the truth from me for years, but finally when I was fourteen she told me about him. He didn't want to know when she told him she was expecting his baby; instead he gave her some money and told her to get rid of it or she would never see him again. She took the money, returned home and started over.' He shrugged.

'That's—that was very hard.' Andi frowned.

Linus gave a humourless smile. 'Or you could say he was just honest.' He shrugged again. 'Even knowing all that, I suppose a part of me still thought that if we actually met each other there would be this moment of instant recognition. Of emotion on both sides.' Linus gave a rueful shake of his head. 'Instead, I felt nothing as I looked at this slightly stooped and balding man well past middle-age. He was a partner in a successful law-firm, but had never married. Was simply a man who had let life pass him by. Who had let my mother pass him by. Believe me, Flora was one hell of a woman,' he assured Andi proudly.

Andi had never imagined Flora Harrison as being anything else. It must have been far from easy for her thirty-six years ago, a single woman raising her child alone.

Successfully raising her child alone. Andi was sure that Flora was the one who had imbued Linus with that same resilience to survive and the determination to succeed. In that moment, Andi felt closer to Linus than ever before.

'I hope you aren't going all dewy-eyed on me.' Linus turned to eye her mockingly. 'The truth of the matter is that I probably succeeded just to spite the bastard,' he acknowledged self-deprecatingly.

'Linus!' Andi found herself smiling in spite of herself.

Linus shrugged unabashed. 'Don't you think it's ironic that the child whose existence he chose to ignore could buy him out a dozen times over?'

No, Andi thought, it was rather sad actually. For Linus, not his father.

Looking back on her own indulged childhood, Andi could only feel grateful for all those years she had spent in the certainty of both her parents' love. 'Tell me about Aunt Mae,' she invited huskily.

Linus smiled affectionately. 'Aunt Mae is extraordinary,' he announced proudly. 'She isn't really my aunt at all, but my mother's. She was already in her fifties and a confirmed spinster when she took me to live with her twenty-one years ago. Ill-equipped, you might think, to take on a grieving fifteen-year-old boy with a considerable chip on his shoulder.' He smiled again at the memory. 'Within minutes of my moving in she had informed me that she wouldn't put up with any of my rebellious ways, that I was to behave myself while in her house or she would know the reason why! I was already seven or eight inches taller than her, and muscled from lifting weights for the last year, and there she stood, like an irate bantam-hen, laying down the law!' He gave an amused shake of his head.

Andi laughed softly at the image this projected. Her own previous mental-image, of Mae Harrison as a round, jolly lady with a bosom as large as her heart, instantly disappeared. 'What did you do?' she prompted curiously.

'Behaved myself, of course. No one messes with my Aunt Mae.'

Andi could hear the deep love and affection in Linus's voice as he spoke of the woman who was actually his great-aunt. She couldn't help feeling admiration for the other woman herself. Not too many women in her position would have taken on the care of her niece's orphaned fifteen-year-old son. Or succeeded so well.

'She sounds wonderful.' Andi nodded.

Linus gave her a sideways glance. 'I wonder if you'll still feel the same way once you've met her.'

Andi had never heard Linus talk about his childhood, or his family, in the way he had in the last few minutes. The knowledge she already had on the subject had all been gleaned from newspaper articles on him over the years. This

personal disclosure gave an intimacy to their relationship that had previously been lacking.

Was that air of intimacy added to because of
what had happened between them last night?
Andi wasn't sure!

She would be a fool if she read any more into
Linus's conversation just now, or his behavior
last night, than was intended. Linus was a man
who lived his life by his own rules, as the
women who came into and then as quickly went
out of his life could testify. Andi would only be
opening herself up to heartache if she were to
read any more into Linus's confidences.
Perhaps he just wanted to explain his relationship with his Aunt Mae before Andi met her.

She drew in a ragged breath. 'I think it's time
we returned to the inn now, don't you? It's
getting colder.'

Linus looked at her between narrowed lids.
He didn't usually talk about his childhood, or the
two women responsible for bringing him up, and
had only done so now because Andi had asked.

No; he would be lying if he said that was why
he had talked of his mother and Aunt Mae so
frankly. For some reason he had wanted Andi,
with her own privileged background, to know,
to understand, why he was the man that he was.

Ordinarily, Linus didn't care one way or the other whether a woman understood him. But he had shared with Andi things he'd never told anybody.

'Okay,' he answered as he turned back towards the inn, the silence between himself and Andi even less comfortable now than it had been earlier.

Why had he told her all that about himself? He never talked about his personal life. At least, he never had before…

'Jim thinks that the snow ploughs should get out this way by later this afternoon,' Linus bit out abruptly.

'That's good.'

He nodded. 'Too late to drive anywhere today, though. But hopefully it means we should be able to continue our journey some time tomorrow.'

'Tomorrow?' The dismay was easily recognizable in Andi's tone.

Linus's mouth twisted as he glanced down at her. 'We have to spend another night at the inn.'

Andi frowned up at him from behind the shield of her dark glasses. 'I can always sleep downstairs in the bar tonight.'

'That's ridiculous and you know it,' Linus

snapped. 'I will try and keep my hands to myself tonight, if you can…'

She bristled angrily, knowing that the brief time of Linus's confidences was most definitely over. 'I have no intention of putting my hands anywhere near you!'

'You did last night…'

'Please don't bring it up.' Andi flushed with embarrassment.

Linus scowled. 'This bickering is even more childish than your suggestion of sleeping in a chair downstairs in the bar tonight.'

Andi scowled. 'It takes two to bicker.'

He drew in a sharp, angry breath. 'God, you're a stubborn woman!'

'It takes one to know one,' she quoted with a saccharin-sweet smile. 'Although in your case it's obviously a stubborn man.'

Linus gave a shake of his head. 'I need to get back to the inn to make some phone calls.'

'Fine,' Andi snapped.

'Absolutely fine,' Linus bit out gratingly.

She raised her brows as he still made no effort to leave. 'Don't let me keep you.'

Andi continued to look up at him for several long seconds before Linus turned sharply on his heel and strode forcefully back towards the inn.

Her breath exhaled slowly, shakily, as she watched him leave. Andi acknowledged that their working relationship of the last year, so easy to maintain during Linus's brief visits to Tarrington Park, was crumbling just as surely as Andi's defences against her growing attraction to him.

CHAPTER SIX

'I'M NOT going to allow you to sit down here all night, you know.' Linus spoke softly as the clock behind the bar struck midnight.

To say things had been strained between he and Andi this evening was an understatement. They had talked to Jennie and Jim, both separately and together, during the evening meal, but never to each other. The landlord and his wife had excused themselves and gone up to bed over an hour ago, leaving their guests to linger downstairs. That hour had been spent in absolute silence.

Putting it bluntly, Linus had had enough of feeling as if he was somehow to blame for the awkwardness between them.

He was used to the women he became involved with occasionally being temperamental if they felt he wasn't paying them enough attention.

But, damn it, Andi worked for him. They

were employer and employee. They weren't supposed to argue. He certainly shouldn't be feeling guilty because of this tension between them.

'*Allow* me, Linus?' Andi repeated softly, one brow raised.

His mouth tightened. 'I am not going to have another argument with you, Andi.'

'Who's arguing?'

Linus tightly clenched his jaw to prevent his knee-jerk reaction to her stubbornness. 'My Aunt Mae told me that a couple should never go to bed with an unresolved argument between them.'

Andi shook her head. 'For one thing, we aren't a couple. For another,' she continued before Linus could interrupt, 'There is no argument between us to resolve.'

Linus gave a disgusted snort. 'Then why aren't you talking to me?'

'I am talking to you.'

'Like I'm some stranger you have to be excessively polite to.'

Andi gave a humourless smile, knowing Linus was right, but unsure what to do about it when she was now so aware of him that she could barely think straight.

She had lingered outside for more than half

an hour longer than Linus this afternoon as she'd tried to get her chaotic thoughts and feelings under control. She had thought she had managed to do that until she'd walked back into the inn and looked at Linus as he sat in the deserted bar talking on the telephone. Just one glance at him had told Andi that no amount of time, or attempts at self-discipline on her part, was going to change the fact that she was so totally aware of Linus now that just looking at him made her pulse race and brought a flush to her cheeks.

The thought of being alone with him in the bedroom again, of lying there and being completely aware of Linus's every breath and movement, was enough to throw her into a panic.

'Just come to bed, Andi!' His hands were clenched at his sides.

Andi felt the warmth in her cheeks even as her breath caught in her throat. *Come to bed, Andi…* Dear God, what longings those words awoke in her.

She had never thought of herself as a particularly sensuous person. How could she when she was still a virgin at the age of twenty-seven? When there hadn't been anyone in her life in the year since David had died?

No doubt that had given Linus the impression that David's death was the reason for her remaining aloof and alone. That she had loved David so deeply that no other man could ever take his place in her heart.

Or her bed.

Andi had faced some hard truths this afternoon as she'd struggled with her newly realized awareness of Linus. One of those truths was that she could no longer even remember what David looked like! She remembered that he'd had blond hair and blue eyes, that playing polo kept him lithe and fit, but the details of his face—the shape of his nose, the curve of his mouth—were memories that eluded her.

She had tried telling herself that the reason for that memory lapse was that she and David hadn't known each other for very long before he'd died; their courtship and engagement had happened so quickly that it wasn't surprising she could no longer remember him clearly. That it was the emotions, what she had felt for David, that were important.

Except Andi couldn't remember those either.

Every time she tried to recall David's face another one would superimpose itself over that image—one with green eyes set in a mocking, ruggedly hewn face. And, when she tried to remember how it had felt to be in love with David, other emotions for another man forced their way to the forefront instead: admiration. Respect. Desire. Most of all desire…

For Linus.

A man who obviously respected and liked women, but women of his mother's age. Of his Aunt Mae's age. Women who were absolutely no threat to the bachelor life he so obviously enjoyed.

Andi wanted Linus to like her. To want her in the same way she wanted him. But the guilt she felt over David was always in the back of her mind.

She wasn't fooling herself into thinking that if a physical relationship between them ever were to happen—as it so easily could have done last night—she would mean any more to Linus than those other women who flitted in and out of his life on such a regular basis.

She wanted him anyway.

She would be damned to no longer being able to work for Linus if she did, damned to living with this ever-increasing aching need if she didn't.

Neither alternative held any appeal.

She gave a weary sigh. 'I just think it's better this way, Linus.'

What way? Linus scowled, frustrated. What thoughts were going through Andi's head as she sat there so quietly and coolly composed? So unreachable.

He had admired Andi's classiness, this style and coolness about her, from the moment they'd first met. Had coveted it, even. Now Linus just wanted to do something, to say something, anything, that would shatter that coolness.

His mouth set grimly. 'How long are you going to continue worshipping at the man's altar, Andi?'

'What?' She gave him a startled look as she sat forward stiffly.

'Simmington-Browne.' Just saying the other man's name made Linus's top lip curl back with distaste. 'How long, Andi—another year? Ten years? The rest of your life, maybe?' His voice had hardened.

Andi gave a dazed shake of her head. 'I don't know what you're talking about.'

'I'm trying to open your eyes to other opportunities,' Linus bit out.

'Stop it, Linus,' she told him shakily, desperately.

'No way,' he rasped firmly, his mouth tight. 'A time of mourning is okay. But what you're doing—the way you live your life.' He gave a decisive shake of his head. 'It isn't normal, Andi. In fact, it's unhealthy!'

Andi stood up, her expression pained. 'You're being unnecessarily cruel, Linus.'

'I'm being truthful.' He scowled darkly. 'How many men have you gone out with in the last year, Andi? How many men have you gone to bed with?'

Andi's breath felt as if it were burning her chest as she put out a hand to tightly grip the back of the chair so that Linus couldn't see how much that hand was shaking in reaction to this unexpected attack. 'I don't have to answer your questions, Linus.' She shook her head, her face very pale.

'Then let me answer them for you,' he bit out disgustedly. 'None, Andi. The answer is none. No dates. Not one single man in your life for the last year.'

Andi shook her head as if to ward off the pained reality of his accusation. 'You can't know that, Linus. You have no idea how I live my life when I'm not in the office with you, the friends that I see.'

'Wrong, Andi,' Linus retorted scathingly. 'Your mother talks to me.'

'My mother?' Andi gasped weakly.

He nodded tersely. 'Marjorie worries about you. She's concerned that you only seem to have work in your life.'

Andi had absolutely no idea that her mother talked to Linus about her. She was aware that he occasionally dropped in and had tea with Marjorie, but Andi hadn't realized that she was often the subject of their conversations!

Her gaze narrowed. 'You aren't seriously suggesting that my mother would rather I have a succession of men in my life in the same way that you have a succession of women in yours?'

His brows rose. 'I don't believe we were talking about my life, Andi.'

'I don't see why not, when you feel no compunction in discussing mine!' Andi was breathing hard in her agitation. 'Why is it that you have a succession of women flitting in and out of your life, Linus?' she challenged tauntingly. 'Could it be because you're as frightened of commitment as your—'

'Choose your words carefully, Andi,' he warned in a dangerously soft voice.

Andi was beyond the caution his words, his whole tense demeanour, advised. 'Several times in the last couple of days you've criticised me for what you view as my unnecessary loyalty to David's memory, so why shouldn't I be allowed to criticise your own lifestyle in the same way? Or the reason for it?'

A nerve pulsed in his tightly clenched jaw. 'I told you those things about my father in confidence!'

'In the same way that my mother talked to you concerning her worries about me, you mean?' she challenged.

'Someone should have told you about the real Simmington-Browne years ago,' he rasped. 'Someone should have told you exactly what kind of a man he really was—' Linus broke off abruptly as he realized exactly where he was going with this conversation. His only excuse— and it was no excuse, really—was that he could never remember feeling this angry before. At anyone. Or anything. 'Forget it, Andi,' he grated dismissively.

'I don't want to forget it, Linus.' Andi's hand on his arm stopped him from turning away. 'What should I have been told about David?' she prompted, confused.

Linus saw the bewilderment reflected in her eyes. In the pallor of her cheeks. And he hated the fact that he was responsible for her dazed expression. He shook his head grimly. 'I should never have started this conversation.'

'Why shouldn't you?' She groaned, frustrated. 'What do you know about David that I don't?'

Linus's mouth firmed. 'I never even met the man.'

Andi's gaze was searching as she looked up at him. 'That doesn't seem to have prevented you from drawing several conclusions about him.'

No, it hadn't, Linus accepted heavily. In truth, he knew more about David Simmington-Browne than he felt comfortable with. 'Let's just go to bed, Andi,' he encouraged lightly.

How could she possibly do that after Linus's hints, accusations, that she hadn't known David as well as she had thought she had? Especially as she had come to the same conclusion herself earlier today when she'd tried to recall David's face. When she'd tried to remember being with him. Tried to remember the love she had felt for him. And failed...

'I need to know, Linus.'

'Why do you?'

She swallowed hard. 'Because I do.' Because she was rapidly falling in love with Linus himself, that was why! If she wasn't already in love with him...

He looked down at her for several minutes before giving a firm shake of his head. 'Not from me, you don't,' he bit out firmly.

'Who else, then?' Andi prompted impatiently. 'Who else is there?'

Linus stared down at her, knowing by the determination in Andi's gaze that she wouldn't rest now until she got to the truth. There was nothing wrong with her knowing the truth about her dead fiancé—Linus just had no intention of being the one to tell her. 'I'm going to bed, Andi,' he told her flatly. 'You can please yourself what you do,' he added dismissively as he shook off her hand on his arm before turning away.

'Linus! I...I'm sorry about my remark earlier—when I implied you avoided commitment in the same way your father did,' she explained reluctantly as Linus frowned his puzzlement. 'I shouldn't have said that.'

'Just for the record, Andi,' he explained, 'I'm not frightened of commitment. I've just never seen the point. If I meet the right woman, then I may consider settling down and getting married, okay? So far I haven't met that woman, but when I do I have every intention of asking her to marry me, okay?'

Andi had a hollow feeling in the pit of her stomach.

When Linus met the right woman he might get married.

Just the thought of Linus marrying this as-yet faceless, nameless woman was enough to make Andi feel ill.

How was she going to feel when Linus married? How would she be able to go on working for him, knowing that at the end of each day he would be going home to his wife, to the bed they shared?

Andi couldn't even bear the thought of it.

The things Linus had implied that she didn't know about David paled into complete insignificance next to the thought of Linus ever getting married.

She shied away from looking too deeply at her feelings for him, knowing it would only result in pain she wasn't ready to deal with. 'Okay,' she accepted huskily.

She looked so small and forlorn as she stood there alone beside the fire, Linus acknowledged with restless impatience. The flames reflected in her hair, turning it to red-gold. That same gold sheen was in the brown depths of her eyes, and the honey glow to her cheeks.

She was so beautiful…

Linus's breath caught in his throat as she returned his gaze. As those brown eyes seemed to turn to liquid gold, and a slight flush coloured her cheeks.

Linus didn't allow himself to think as he took the three strides that took him back to Andi's side; as he lifted a hand and cupped it lightly against the warmth of her cheek; as he gazed down into the honey-brown depths of her eyes.

Andi gazed right back at him. Not challengingly, but questioningly.

It was Linus's cue to stop this right now. To bring a halt to something that would ultimately lead to disaster. Except he couldn't do it. He wanted to kiss Andi. Wanted to do more than kiss her. But he would settle for tasting her. For feeling the warm response of her mouth beneath his. For now…

Linus lowered his head slowly, all the time holding Andi's gaze with his own, his groan completely involuntary as his lips came into contact with hers. She tasted so good! So sweet, like nectar. 'Open your mouth for me, Andi,' he groaned huskily against her lips. 'Let me in!' he encouraged achingly even as his tongue moved in a light caress against the softness of her lips.

Lips that parted invitingly as Andi stepped fully into his arms, her own arms moving up to curve about his shoulders as her fingers became entangled in the dark thickness of the hair at his nape.

It was all the encouragement Linus needed to deepen the kiss, his lips hard and demanding against hers as he dipped his tongue into her honeyed sweetness.

Andi trembled as the thrust of Linus's tongue claimed her mouth, seeking, possessing, taking. Igniting.

She pressed close against him as the kiss deepened hungrily, her breasts highly sensitized as they came into contact with the hardness of Linus's chest, that hardness abrasive against her aroused nipples and sending hot rivulets of arousal down to her already-heated thighs.

Linus's hand left the curve of her cheek to travel slowly, caressingly down over her breast, the dip of her waist and lower still. His fingers curved over her bottom to pull her even closer against his arousal, the hard feel of him there causing a wild rush of pleasure that had Andi wet and aching within seconds as she moved restlessly against him.

That ache deepened to near pain as his hand moved to the curve of her breast, cupping, lightly squeezing, the soft pad of his thumb unerringly finding the thrust of her nipple against the soft wool of her jumper.

Andi groaned softly as the whole of her body seemed to melt, that ache between her thighs becoming a heated throb, her fingers clinging to Linus's shoulders as his mouth left hers to trail down her throat to the deep hollows beneath, tongue dipping, tasting.

Her neck arched in invitation, supplication, as Linus moved back slightly to sit on the arm of the chair before pushing her jumper up above her breasts. One hand moved to cup and caress even as his head lowered, and he suckled the other fiery tip into the heat and moisture of his mouth.

Andi's legs buckled at this dual assault upon her senses, the smooth caress of the pad of Linus's thumb and the rasping caress of his tongue. It was…sublime. Ecstasy. Unlike anything she had ever known before.

Her fingers were tangled in Linus's hair as she held him to her, unwilling for this pleasure to ever stop. Her gasp became a groan as Linus turned the attention of his mouth to her other breast, licking, tasting, before suckling deeply.

Linus felt Andi's restlessness as her thighs pressed urgently against his, his own arousal so hard and tight it was almost painful as he felt the heat of Andi's need.

Her stomach was flat and hot as he loosened the button on her denims before slipping his hand beneath, her curls soft and silky as he sought the centre of her need, lightly caressing with his fingers as he found that hardened nub. Stroking her. Once. Twice. He was able to feel her quivers of release on his third stroke, and Linus suckled harder on her breast as he took Andi over the edge. She came in spasm after spasm as release shook her heated slickness.

Andi felt herself coming apart. Disintegrating. Shattering into a thousand, a million, pieces as her body convulsed and shook in a burning release that was beyond imagining, seemingly never-ending.

Until reality hit her with the force of a blow.

Her forehead rested on Linus's shoulder as she became aware of her surroundings. Of the softness of his sweater cool against her heated skin. The air feeling cool too against her bared breasts. Both his arms were lightly about her waist now.

Andi shivered, not with cold but with reaction. What had she just done? What had she just allowed to happen? She couldn't have stopped that if she had tried; she had been totally lost from the moment Linus had begun to kiss her.

Linus!

What must he think of her?

He had kissed her more intimately than any other man. Had touched her more intimately than any other man. Had given her more pleasure...

Linus felt it as Andi began to shiver in reaction, his arms tightening about her as she would have moved sharply away from him. 'You were beautiful, Andi,' he told her gruffly. 'Absolutely beautiful.'

She raised her head slowly, eyes dark and shadowed, the hollows in her cheeks more pronounced beneath those shadowy depths. Her expression was one of regret as well as embarrassment.

Linus groaned softly as he saw that regret in her eyes. 'Don't, Andi...'

'Don't what?' Her voice broke emotionally as she pulled out of his arms, turned away and straightened her clothing. 'Don't feel embarrassed? Mortified?' Her voice rose angrily as she turned back to look at him with sparkling eyes. 'How do you want me to feel, Linus?' she challenged harshly. 'Warm and soft? Girlish and coy? Or will just *grateful* do?'

Linus could feel the nerve pulsing in his cheek as he fought to contain his own anger. Anything he and Andi said to each other now was going to sound wrong. Better to walk away from this before one or both of them said something they were going to regret. As he already regretted letting this situation between them get so out of control...

'Go to bed, Andi,' he rasped as he turned away from her. 'I'll sleep down here tonight. We'll talk in the morning.'

Andi stared at the hard rigidity of Linus's back, wondering what he was thinking. What he thought of her. Whatever it was, it couldn't be any worse than what she thought of herself. She wondered now how everything was going to change.

'What is there left for us to talk about?' she bit out. 'Whether or not you want me to give the three months' notice required in my contract, or whether you would prefer me to just leave immediately?'

Linus's eyes had narrowed to icy green slits as he turned to look at her. 'Who said anything about your leaving?'

Andi gave a disbelieving snort. 'I believe you did, when you told me you never become personally involved with your female employees! Unless, of course, you don't class what just happened as being "personally involved"?' She breathed shakily, wondering if she could possibly feel any worse than she already did. She trembled just at the memory of the intimacies they had shared. 'How can we continue working together now?'

His mouth tightened. 'Do you want us to continue working together?'

She grimaced. 'I don't think what I want comes into it, do you?'

'Oh, I think that it does.' He nodded slowly, pale gaze unreadable.

Andi closed her eyes briefly before raising her lids to look at him once again. 'I want just now not to have happened,' she muttered gruffly. 'I want to go back to as we were before,' she finished.

Linus gave a humourless smile. 'And if that proves to be impossible?'

She swallowed hard. 'Then I'll have to consider leaving.'

He continued to look at her for several long minutes before nodding abruptly. 'In that case,

I suggest we give resuming our previous relationship another go. I don't see the need for your resignation.'

How different this could have been if Linus had loved her, Andi wished achingly. If Linus loved her as she was starting to love him...

Because she did love him. She had absolutely no doubts about that now. She knew she could never have behaved in the way she just had, never have responded in that way, if she wasn't already in love with Linus.

Just as Andi knew that the only way she could stay in Linus's life was if he never knew that she loved him.

'I still can't believe—' Andi broke off with a self-conscious groan. 'Jim or Jennie could have walked in on us a few minutes ago!'

'But they didn't.' His eyes flashed.

'More by luck than judgement!' Andi's eyes flared darkly, knowing that anger was probably a safer emotion than the complete devastation she really felt.

'Stop beating yourself up, Andi, and just go to bed,' Linus rasped wearily.

One look at the grimness of his expression told Andi that Linus didn't want to talk about this any more tonight, either. If ever!

Which suited her perfectly. Andi could imagine nothing more cringe-making, more embarrassing, than discussing her complete lack of control a few minutes ago.

A lack of control that still made her body tremble and quake with remembered pleasure…

'Fine.' She nodded abruptly. 'I—I'll see you in the morning, then.'

'No doubt,' Linus bit out.

Andi hesitated only long enough to give him one last, lingering glance before hurrying from the room and up the stairs to the bedroom, closing the door sharply behind her, wishing she could as easily close the door on her memories.

How would she ever be able to so much as look at Linus again without those memories blazing between them?

She would certainly never be able to look at Linus again without knowing that she was falling for him…

CHAPTER SEVEN

'IT WAS kind of Jim and Jennie to pack lunch for us,' Andi ventured softly later the next morning as she turned to wave to the landlord and his wife as they stood in the doorway of the inn, watching them leave. The snow-plough had done its job and cleared the minor road earlier this morning now that the major roads were driveable.

Linus slanted her a brief glance. 'And you could use a little kindness right now, hmm?' He watched as a becoming blush coloured her cheeks. Cheeks that until a few minutes ago had been deathly pale.

Not that Linus felt much better. He hadn't slept well the previous night, and that lack of sleep owed nothing to the uncomfortableness of the chair he'd slept in and more to the fact that he couldn't get Andi out of his head. Kissing her. How she had felt. How soft and creamy her skin was. How responsive her body was to the slightest caress. Of how she had completely come apart in his arms.

He had still been able to taste her. To feel her. Her skin had felt so satin-smooth. Her breasts had fit perfectly into his hands. Her curls had been soft and silky to the touch as he'd sought and found the centre of her arousal. Andi had been so responsive, so completely beautiful, as he'd felt her climax against his stroking fingers.

Linus hadn't been able to get the memory of that from his head.

He still couldn't.

So much so that all Linus wanted to do right now was take Andi to the nearest bed and finish what they had started last night.

He wanted to see her naked. He wanted to know if those silky-soft curls were as golden as her hair. Wanted to touch and kiss the petalled rose between her thighs, to drive Andi over that edge with the touch of his lips and tongue. Most of all, Linus wanted to bury himself inside that rosy moistness, to stroke himself inside her again and again until they both found release.

In the circumstances it was probably as well that he had to concentrate so hard on his driving. The roads were still slightly icy despite having been gritted overnight. Although that didn't stop his thoughts from constantly returning to the previous evening...

What the hell had happened between the two of them?

Linus had always been aware of Andi as a coolly beautiful and accomplished woman—it was one of the reasons he had employed her. But last night Andi had been so much more than that. The coolness had completely melted to reveal a woman with physical passions that ran as fiercely as his own. She had been so hot and responsive, almost wild in her pleasure.

Had Andi reacted in the same way in Simmington-Browne's arms?

Jealousy wasn't an emotion Linus recognized. In the same way he didn't recognize possessiveness. He had never had any use for either emotion.

And yet just the thought of any other man bringing Andi to the same release he had last night filled Linus with anger.

'Perhaps you don't like my particular brand of kindness?' he rasped insultingly.

Andi drew in a sharp breath at what she was sure was Linus's deliberate attempt to humiliate her. What other reason could he have for reminding her so forcibly, so tauntingly, of what had happened between them the previous evening?

A memory she had been trying so hard to forget but couldn't...

How could she possibly forget that Linus had kissed her, touched her, aroused her?

Well maybe Andi would never be able to forget any of those things, but she certainly didn't have to let Linus know about them. 'There's no perhaps about it,' she came back coldly.

Linus shot her a scathing glance. 'You didn't seem so sure of that last night!'

This time Andi's gasp was audible, and the colour once again faded from her cheeks.

He sighed heavily. 'I didn't get much sleep last night, okay?'

Andi accepted this probably wasn't the best time in the world for them to discuss the events of last night—she doubted there would ever be a good time.

Although she was curious as to why Linus hadn't slept well either...

Now that she looked at him, Andi could see that lack of sleep in the heaviness of Linus's eyes, with their dark shadows beneath, and in the grim set of his mouth and jaw.

Could it be that Linus had been as affected by their passionate clinch as she had? Oh, she knew Linus had been aroused—the physical evidence of that had been all too obvious as he'd moulded her body against his—but had it been more than that for both of them?

No, of course it hadn't, Andi answered herself harshly. Linus was a 'bed 'em and leave 'em' man, and he never allowed any of the softer emotions into those relationships. If Linus hadn't slept well last night it had to be because he had found the chair uncomfortable, not because he had been thinking about her.

'Perhaps it would be better if we didn't talk,' he suggested practically.

Easier said than done, Linus realized unhappily as they continued the rest of the drive to his Aunt Mae's in silence. A silence far removed from the easy companionship that had existed between them before last night.

But how could it be any different when Linus was completely aware of everything about Andi this morning? Of the soft sweep of her hair as it flowed loosely about her shoulders; the pale oval of her face; those brown eyes, dark and unfathomable. The way the brown sweater and denims fitted over the soft curves of her body. The delicate perfume she always wore.

Strange; Linus had never particularly noticed that perfume before, but now he realized it was one he always associated with Andi: light, slightly floral, almost elusive.

Like Andi herself.

Whether he liked it or not, last night had changed something between them. Something tangible.

But changed it into what, Linus had no idea…

'My Aunt Mae doesn't bite,' Linus assured her mockingly when Andi joined him at the back of the Range Rover as he took their luggage out of the boot.

Andi shot him an irritated look. She doubted whether the older woman could fail to pick up on the tension that undoubtedly existed between Linus and her. A tension that surely shouldn't exist between her nephew and the woman who was his PA.

'Very funny,' Andi muttered as she picked up her overnight bag, before turning away.

Just in time to see a small, wiry lady with iron-grey hair pulled back in a no-nonsense bun, and wearing a floral pinafore over her woollen dress. She came out of the small cottage, eyes the same green as Linus's fixed affectionately on her great-nephew as she hurried down the pathway to join them.

Andi stood politely to one side as Linus turned to swing his Aunt Mae up in his arms in a hug that would have crushed a less robust woman.

'Put me down, ye wee heathen, and introduce me to my guest!' his aunt finally instructed, the sternness of her expression belied by the tears of pleasure that glistened in her eyes as she looked proudly at Linus.

Linus's grin was mischievous as he slowly lowered the elderly lady back onto her slippered feet. 'Aunt Mae, this is Andrea Buttonfield. Andi, my aunt, Mae Harrison.'

'Call me Mae,' the elderly lady invited warmly as she took Andi's hand in a surprisingly strong grip, at the same time as that green gaze swept over Andi with the astuteness she had suspected, and dreaded, would be there.

'Andi,' she returned lightly as she kept her expression deliberately neutral under that piercing gaze.

'Come inside and have some tea and cake,' the older woman invited with brisk warmth as she turned and led the way back into the cottage.

'I'll just bring the bags in, shall I?' Linus muttered.

'It's one of the few things men are good for,' his aunt returned without so much as a turn of her head.

'Don't put ideas in Andi's head!' he called after them dryly.

Once inside, Andi sat, slightly dazed. She felt as if she were back in the eye of the same storm of Linus's arrival at Tarrington Park two days ago. Mae Harrison was every bit as astute as Andi had thought she might be. But she was also much more—warm. Kind. Obviously incredibly proud of her great-nephew, the fierce love she felt for him shining in those wonderful eyes so like Linus's own.

'So, what do you think?'

Andi gave a start before she turned sharply to look at Linus, as he stood in the doorway grinning across at her. 'What do I think about what?' she came back guardedly.

'Aunt Mae.' His grin widened as he came further into the room; his earlier look of strain seemed to have completely dissipated, and he stood in front of the blazing fire to warm himself.

He looked different in these surroundings, Andi realized. Less the arrogant Linus Harrison, successful entrepreneur, and more boyish Linus Harrison, Mae Harrison's orphaned great-nephew.

Andi suddenly felt her cheeks warm, and not from the heat of the fire. Not because she was shocked by the sentiment but because of how close she and Linus had come to crossing the boundary of their relationship the evening before.

'Here we are,' his aunt announced briskly as she came in carrying the laden tea-tray.

Linus crossed the room to take the tray from his aunt's unresisting fingers, before he placed it on the small cloth-covered table at the back of the room that served as dining room as well as sitting room.

This cottage had seemed very small to Linus when he'd moved here as a teenager, the low ceilings completely unsuitable for his height even then.

But Linus had come to love this cottage and the rugged beauty of its surrounding country-side almost as much as he had come to love his Aunt Mae. 'Is pouring tea another use we men have?' he teased his deceptively brisk aunt; beneath her gruff exterior, Mae had a heart almost as big as she was.

'I trust you'll excuse my nephew, Andi.' His

aunt frowned at him disapprovingly as she made herself comfortable in the armchair opposite Andi's. 'I assure you, I never brought him up to be so disrespectful.'

Linus grinned, unconcerned. 'I'll take that as a yes.'

Andi was very much enjoying the exchange between Linus and his aunt, and doubted very much that he ever got the better of the sharp-tongued Mae Harrison.

Although Andi was less sure about seeing a side of Linus that she had never realized existed. A lighthearted, teasing side that hid the wealth of love he obviously felt for the woman who had taken him into her home and her heart when he'd been fifteen.

'So, Andi.' Mae Harrison drew her attention away from Linus. 'How long have you and Linus known each other? If I don't ask you, I'll never know,' she added confidingly. 'He never tells me anything about his private life.'

Andi gave the older woman a startled look. 'Oh, but—'

'Andi isn't part of my private life, Aunt Mae,' Linus informed her dryly as he handed the women two of the cups of tea he had poured, raising one dark brow in Andi's direction as he

saw the heated colour enter her cheeks. 'Cake?'
His expression was deceptively innocent as he
gave Andi an empty plate before offering the
plate containing his Aunt Mae's fruit cake, no
doubt baked especially for the occasion.

Andi seemed slightly in a daze as she
absently took a piece of the fruit cake. 'You
seem to be under some sort of misapprehen-
sion as to my identity, Miss Harrison.'

'Now, didn't I ask you to call me Mae?'
Linus's aunt rebuked her gently, at the same
time shooting him a questioning glance.

Linus easily guessed the reason for Mae's
puzzlement; as he had already explained to
Andi, she really wasn't what his aunt had been
expecting from Linus's own description of his
PA as being 'prim, officious and efficient'. A
description that until last night he had genuinely
thought applied to Andi. But not any more...

He frowned slightly. 'Andi is my PA, Aunt
Mae,' he supplied abruptly as he turned away
to collect his own cup of tea and piece of cake,
before sitting down on the foot-stool beside his
aunt's chair.

Nevertheless, he sensed Mae's thoughtful
gaze fixed on him for several seconds. De-
servedly so, considering his previous comments

about Andi had given his aunt the impression that she was a much older woman, an older woman who he had no more interest in seducing than she had in being seduced.

He had found the situation amusing when he'd told Andi yesterday. Now, with his aunt looking at him so interestedly, Linus felt far less amused.

'Andi seems to have finished her tea, so perhaps I could show her up to her room so that she can freshen up after our journey?' he suggested lightly, knowing by Andi's slightly dazed expression as she looked down at the empty cup in her hand and the plate on her knee that she had probably consumed both without even being aware of doing so. 'I take it Andi has my old bedroom and I'm in the box room?' he asked his aunt lightly as he met her searching gaze with one of deliberate blandness.

An expression that obviously didn't fool her for one moment. 'Do that.' His aunt nodded.

Andi was well aware that there was some sort of exchange going on between aunt and nephew beneath the surface-politeness of their conversation. Just as she was aware that she was the subject of that exchange. But how much Mae Harrison knew, or had guessed, about Andi's relationship with Linus she wasn't sure…

'There's really no need for Linus to give up his bedroom for me,' she assured her brightly. 'I'm sure I would be perfectly comfortable in the box room.'

'I wouldn't hear of it,' Mae Harrison told her decisively as she stood up. 'Never turn down an act of self-sacrifice on a man's part, Andi,' she reproved lightly. 'They have things far too much their own way in this world as it is.'

Andi gave a rueful smile. 'Linus very generously gave up his bed for me last night—' She broke off abruptly, fiery colour entering her cheeks at the realization that she and Linus had been stranded at the inn for two nights and not one. She shot Linus a beseeching glance to cover her obvious mistake.

A glance he returned with mocking amusement. 'Andi meant, of course, that due to the fact that the inn had only one spare bedroom I've had to spend the last two nights sleeping in a chair,' he drawled.

'Quite right too,' his aunt approved briskly. 'It's nice to know that not all my teaching went in one ear and out the other! Well, don't keep Andi standing there; away with ye and show her to the room she's to use.'

Andi still felt slightly disorientated as she

followed Linus up the narrow staircase to the bedrooms above. She had known this visit to Linus's aunt was going to be awkward the moment he'd mentioned it to her, but it was so much worse than Andi had even imagined it would be. She couldn't hide the feelings she felt for the dynamic Linus Harrison, a man who was as arrogant as he was successful. But the Linus Harrison she had seen the last couple of days— the man who was Mae Harrison's nephew, who not only respected his aunt but obviously adored her—was so much more endearing.

'Sorry, it's a little cold up here.' Linus looked down at Andi as he saw her shiver when they entered the room that had been his bedroom during his teens and early twenties.

Andi gave him a wan smile. 'I— Please don't linger up here on my account. I'm sure that you and your aunt have a lot of catching up to do.'

Linus already knew that most of that 'catching up' would be about Andi herself. 'Andi…'

'I'll come down in a few minutes,' she assured him huskily, her gaze not meeting his as she looked about the bedroom instead.

Linus frowned down at her. 'Andi?'

'Linus, would you mind giving me some time to freshen up?' she asked as she looked up at him. 'This last couple of days, travelling up to Scotland and then getting stranded in the snow, has been quite hard.'

Hard? That wasn't quite the description that Linus would have used concerning the last two days. But perhaps to Andi, forced by circumstances into such close proximity with him, that was exactly what it had been.

Perhaps he shouldn't have brought Andi to Scotland with him at all.

'Fine,' he bit out. 'There's only the one small bathroom, I'm afraid.'

'I'm sure I'll manage, Linus,' she concluded.

He nodded. 'It's just down the hallway on the right. Come downstairs when you're ready.' He gave another nod before leaving.

Andi sat down abruptly on the single bed as she heard Linus returning down stairs, not sure she would ever be 'ready' to face him again, let alone the searching gaze of his aunt.

But as she looked about the bedroom that had once been Linus's she didn't think she would be able to remain up here for too long, either.

The walls were mainly covered in posters. Not of the scantily-clad females she might have expected from the teenager and young man Linus had been when he'd lived here; instead there were dozens of posters on rugby. The players. The fixtures. The stadiums.

The single bookcase beside the bed held a much-read collection of paperbacks. His taste was eclectic as it ranged from the classics to murder-mysteries, and of course rugby. Even the duvet cover on the bed Andi sat on was styled in the colours of the Scottish rugby team!

Everywhere Andi looked she was surrounded by the evidence of Linus's years of living here, by his presence.

And this was the bedroom she was expected to sleep in tonight!

CHAPTER EIGHT

'COME in and sit by the range where it's warm,' Mae Harrison invited as Andi hesitated in the kitchen doorway.

The kitchen was cosy and warm, and filled with the smell of food cooking as Mae fried onions in a pan on top of the range. A wooden rocking-chair was placed to one side, obviously one that the elderly lady often used herself, the cushions old and faded.

The homeliness of the cottage was such a contrast to the apartment Linus occasionally used at the top of Tarrington Park. His taste there ran to large, comfortable furniture in the sitting room, and a streamlined kitchen in black and yellow with all the modern electrical-conveniences at his disposal.

'The floor is original, but Linus fitted these units himself,' the elderly lady announced proudly as she saw Andi's admiring gaze on the pale-stone floor and mellowed-oak cupboards. 'He wanted to install a new-fangled gas Aga too.' Mae wrinkled her nose scathingly. 'But, as I told him, I've had this old wood-burning range for over forty years and I know its foibles as well as it knows mine!'

Andi smiled. 'Is there anything I can do to help?' she offered politely.

'Just sit yourself down,' the older woman assured her briskly. 'I'm making Linus's favourite—cottage pie,' she confided as she saw Andi's interest in what she was doing.

'I didn't know that.' On the occasions her mother had invited Linus to dine with the two of them at the gate house, he'd seemed to enjoy eating whatever was put in front of him.

There were a lot of things that Andi hadn't known about Linus before accompanying him on this visit to his homeland...

'Och aye,' Mae confirmed affectionately. 'Of course, he probably eats all that fancy food when he's in England, but whenever he comes home it's a cottage pie he always asks for. I'll never tell him so, of course, but he's a good wee laddy,' she added warmly. 'Wild and angry with the world when he first came here to live with me, of course.' She frowned. 'But what teenager wouldn't be when the mother he adored had just died?'

Andi murmured something appropriate, not sure she wanted to hear any of this. After last night, it was much easier for her to think of Linus only as the rich and successful man who used and discarded women, rather than to be told how wonderful he was by the elderly great-aunt who had helped to bring him up.

'Linus told me how you've had your own share of tragedy, so of course you would understand the anger he was feeling all those years ago.'

Andi looked up sharply to find herself the focus of a shrewd green gaze. 'Sorry…?' Which 'tragedy' was Mae Harrison referring to?

The death of Andi's father? Or the death of her fiancé in the same car accident?

'Perhaps I shouldn't have mentioned it,' the elderly woman murmured apologetically, as she saw Andi's pained confusion. 'I just thought— Maybe I just wanted you to know why Linus is the man that he is…'

Which man was that? Andi wondered, slightly dazed. The man who had helped Andi to turn her mother's life around after the death of her father and the discovery of those horren-dous debts, by offering them the gate house as their home? The same man who had employed a housekeeper in order to make her mother's life easier and to be a companion to Marjorie now that Andi was expected to go away on business with him? The almost-lover of the previous evening? The affectionate nephew he was to Mae? Or the man who had become successful despite—or as Linus himself claimed simply *to* spite—the father who had denied him even before his birth?

Linus was all of those things.

'He's very successful,' she said noncommittally.

'Aye, he is that,' Mae murmured approvingly. 'Through sheer, hard work, mind. He's never cheated, or lied, or done any of those things that other big businessmen seem to do to get ahead,' she added sternly as if Andi might ever have thought otherwise.

Having worked with Linus for the last year, Andi had no reason to disagree with the older woman's claims. She knew it was because Linus was the man that he was that so many of the same building contractors and craftsmen worked for him time and again. Linus was that rare thing in business nowadays—as hardworking as the people he employed. In fact, when Linus had visited Tarrington Park during the alterations, Andi had often seen him discarding his jacket and tie and setting to work himself if necessary.

'Linus has never forgotten his roots,' snorted Mae.

'Singing my praises again, Aunt Mae?' Linus mocked as he opened the kitchen door and allowed a blast of cold air to blast into the room with him. He was carrying a stack of wood across the room and dropped it into the basket beside the range before straightening. 'I hope you haven't been regaling Andi with any of the deeds of my misspent youth?' he added teasingly.

He hadn't expected Andi to come downstairs before he returned from chopping the wood, and wondered now exactly what Aunt Mae had been talking about in his absence. If it was anything like the twenty questions about Andi that his aunt had given him a short time ago, then he felt sorry for her!

'You didn't have a misspent youth,' his aunt retorted sternly. 'I would never have allowed it while you were living under my roof!'

'That's true,' Linus drawled. 'She was worse than Sherlock Holmes,' he confided in Andi dryly. 'Knew what I'd done before I'd even done it. I tried one cigarette—one,' he emphasized. 'When I was sixteen. And as soon as I walked back in the door she sat me down in that rocking chair you're sitting in now and gave me a lecture on the perils of the dreaded weed. With graphic details, I might add. I've never touched another once since!'

'A good thing too.' His aunt nodded unrepentantly. 'Now, take Andi into the sitting room and offer her a glass of sherry before supper so that I can get on with my cooking.'

Andi frowned slightly. 'I hope I haven't been too much of a nuisance.'

'You haven't been a nuisance at all,' Mae assured her briskly. 'I simply can't abide having a man in my kitchen.'

Linus chuckled softly as he opened the door for Andi to precede him into the adjoining sitting-room.

Andi took the glass he handed her, taking a sip of the sherry before answering him, grateful for the feel of the warming liquid inside her.

'I really wish you hadn't brought me here, Linus.' She looked uncomfortable.

'Why not?' Linus rasped irritably as he moved away from her to stand beside the fire.

'I realize the cottage isn't quite what you're used to by way of accommodation, but—'

'That is completely unfair, Linus!' Andi protested indignantly. 'The cottage is charming. As is your aunt.'

He scowled darkly. 'That would appear to leave only me you aren't comfortable with…?'

'It isn't you either.' She sighed impatiently. *Well…not exactly.*

'Then what is the problem?' He threw his own sherry to the back of his throat before crossing the room to refill his glass.

Andi turned away, wondering how she could best explain herself without revealing too much of her inner turmoil. Being here like this with Linus, in the only real home he had known since he was fifteen, was playing havoc with her need to hold herself distant from him. After last night there didn't seem to be any other option open to her, and yet it was impossible to remain detached, removed, while in the presence of his aunt and the easy affection that existed between the two of them.

Especially as Mae Harrison's shrewd, green gaze seemed to have noticed there was something other than the relationship of employer and employee between them. What other reason could the other woman have for talking to her about Linus so defensively?

'What did you tell your aunt about me, Linus?' she asked.

'What do you think I told her?' he rasped, his eyes narrowed in warning. 'You don't imagine that I've told her what happened between us last night?'

'No, of course not!' Colour burned Andi's cheeks. 'I simply— She wasn't talking to me just now as if I were your employee.' Andi shook her head, frowning. 'I feel somehow as if I'm here under false pretences.'

'That's rubbish, Andi, and you know it.' Linus crossed the room in two strides, standing dangerously close now. 'I think you're projecting your own feelings of awkwardness onto Aunt Mae.'

'I am?' Andi blinked up at him, wishing he wasn't standing quite so close—so close that she could see the gold flecks in the green of his eyes. So close that she had only to reach out and... 'I really shouldn't be here, Linus,' she insisted firmly, as her hand tightened about the sherry glass she held and her other hand clenched at her side. 'This is your home. Your Aunt Mae is your only close family.'

'Marjorie is your only close family,' he

pointed out grimly. 'That's never stopped me from visiting her.'

'That's different, and you know it.' Andi gave an impatient shake of her head. 'You own the gate house, Linus,' she explained at his questioning look. 'You have a perfect right to visit it whenever you choose.'

'But I don't visit the gate house, Andi, I visit Marjorie.'

Andi was well aware of that. Just as she knew how much her mother enjoyed Linus's visits. Only Andi, it seemed, was uncomfortable with the easy familiarity that had developed between Linus and her mother. Or with this visit to Linus's Aunt Mae.

'Never mind.' She turned away dismissively. 'You obviously don't understand.'

Linus studied her, frustrated, for several seconds. The soft curtain of her hair partly obscured Andi's face, but what he could see of her features looked far from happy.

Because she really didn't feel comfortable being at his aunt's home? Or because of something else?

Andi had made it pretty plain, both then and this morning, that she would rather last night had never happened, that she just wanted to forget about it. But had she? Had he? Somehow Linus doubted that very much, on both counts.

Andi had been so responsive in his arms the previous evening, so absolutely, stunningly beautiful in her pleasure, that Linus doubted he would ever be able to put that memory from his mind.

'Help me to understand, Andi,' he invited huskily as he moved even closer to her, so close he could feel the warmth of her body and smell the elusiveness of her perfume. His own body hardened in response to that dual assault upon his senses.

Her gaze was wary as she looked up at him. It was a wariness Linus found even more displeasing than the coolness he had felt emanating towards him all day.

Andi had been right in her assertion that the two of them working together in future was going to be difficult, Linus accepted grimly. Worse than difficult—perhaps impossible...?

Linus realized that he didn't regret a single thing about last night, and doubted that he ever would. In fact, right now, he wanted nothing more than to repeat the experience. More than repeat it—he wanted Andi fully. Wanted to bury himself inside her. Deep, deep inside her as he joined her in that mindless pleasure.

At which point she would definitely hand in her notice.

Andi's gaze was still wary as she looked up at Linus. What was he thinking? Whatever it was, the thought obviously displeased him, as his mouth tightened grimly.

'Forget I asked,' he bit out, before moving abruptly away from her. 'Just bear with me for tonight and I promise that I will get you away from here as quickly as is polite tomorrow morning.'

He really didn't understand, Andi accepted heavily. How could he when it was Andi's own emotions that were so raw? How could he possibly understand that a part of her, an increasingly large part of her, so wished that she were here with Linus as something other than his PA? That he had brought her here to introduce her to his Aunt Mae as—what? His girlfriend? His future wife?

Now she really was being fanciful, Andi recognized heavily.

No, Linus was right; the sooner they left here tomorrow, the better she would feel.

'Come in,' Andi called softly in answer to the light tap on her bedroom door—Linus's bedroom! door—her eyes widening when it was Linus himself who entered the room and closed the door quietly behind him. She had believed it to be Aunt Mae, come to check that she was comfortable before going to bed herself.

Andi instinctively clutched the bedclothes to her throat as she looked across the room at Linus, his height and the broad width of his shoulders instantly dwarfing his childhood bedroom.

Surprisingly, it had been a pleasant evening, the food and Mae Harrison's presence helping to alleviate the tension that now existed between Andi and Linus. On both sides.

What did Linus want now? What could they possibly have to say to each other that hadn't already been said?

Linus's mouth twisted derisively as he easily read the apprehension in Andi's expression and the way she clutched the duvet to her so tightly her knuckles showed white. 'Don't look so worried, Andi, I'm hardly going to want to continue where we left off last night with my Aunt Mae just down the hallway!'

Her apprehensive gaze turned to a glare. 'We aren't going to "continue where we left off last night" here or anywhere else!'

Linus shrugged as he crossed the room to

stand beside the bed, his gaze lightly mocking. 'Are you sure about that?'

'Very sure!'

'Isn't that a little selfish of you?'

Andi shook her head, frowning. 'I don't understand.'

'Only one of us found release last night, Andi—and it wasn't me!' Linus reminded her dryly.

Andi's eyes widened even as the colour faded from her cheeks at the embarrassment she felt at being reminded of her complete lack of control the previous evening.

'What do you want, Linus?' she prompted, afraid he would see her embarrassment.

'Why, to see if my aunt's guest is completely comfortable, of course,' he drawled. 'Are you?' he prompted huskily.

She had been until Linus had entered the bedroom, Andi acknowledged. Now her earlier tension had returned with a vengeance!

And not just her tension…

Andi felt at a distinct disadvantage lying here in bed, with only the duvet to cover her as Linus looked down at her with lazily appreciative eyes. She felt surprisingly hot; her breasts were tingling, the nipples hard and sensitized, and a burning ache between her thighs. An ache she knew Linus could so easily satisfy…

She swallowed hard. 'I'm fine, thank you.'

He gave a mocking inclination of his head. 'There's nothing I can do to make you feel more…comfortable?'

Her eyes flashed darkly as colour filled her cheeks again. 'Absolutely nothing!'

'No?'

'No! Linus, what are you doing?' she demanded indignantly as he sat on the side of the bed, his weight pulling the duvet tightly across her body, the material chafing across her roused breasts and almost making her groan out loud.

What was wrong with her? She wasn't this person; had never been this person. Had never felt this way before, with David or any other man. Had never been a woman who only had to look at a man—a certain man—and want to throw off all her clothes and offer her body.

She shook her head determinedly. 'You have to go, Linus!'

'Have to, Andi?' he teased, edging close to her.

'Don't you see—' She broke off as he lifted a hand and curved that warmth against one of her heated cheeks. 'Don't, Linus,' she groaned achingly as he began to lower his head towards hers.

Linus knew that he shouldn't. But he had to; he couldn't help himself.

How could he not kiss Andi when she lay there looking so sexy? When her every glance—although Andi probably wasn't even aware of it—was inviting him to do so?

Linus deliberately held her gaze with his as he came to a halt with his lips mere centimetres away from hers, the warmth of their breath intermingling as he looked deeply into her eyes.

He had told himself earlier that he was only coming to his old bedroom to check that Andi was okay; that once he had done that he would leave. One look at her—her golden hair spilling across the pillow beneath her, those dark eyes as warm as chocolate—and Linus knew he had only been fooling himself with that excuse, that he had come to Andi's bedroom for one reason and one reason only: he hadn't been able to stay away.

Why hadn't he? What was it about Andi that drew him to her like a siren's lure?

Until Linus had the answer to those questions, he knew he would be wise to resist that lure.

He straightened abruptly. 'You're right,' he

grated as he stood up and moved sharply away from the bed. 'I should go.'

'Linus?'

'What?'

He looked so angry, Andi acknowledged heavily. With her? Or with himself? Andi wasn't sure; she only knew that whatever emotion had prompted him almost to kiss her a few seconds ago had now been replaced with cold dismissal.

She blinked. 'Why are you so angry, Linus?'

His mouth twisted self-effacingly. 'It's nothing a cold shower won't cure.'

Her eyes widened as his meaning became clear. Linus was as aroused by her as she was by him. Even here, in his aunt's cottage, Linus wanted her.

She gave a sad shake of her head. 'We really need to talk, Linus.'

'What is there to talk about?' he came back tauntingly. 'You're still hung up on a dead man, and I'm not masochistic enough to want to compete with his memory!'

Andi gave a pained expression. 'You're being unnecessarily cruel, Linus.'

Was he? Probably, Linus accepted harshly. It was incredibly frustrating not being able to tell Andi what a bastard her fiancé had really been. How their whole engagement had been nothing but a lie. Well, Linus *could* tell Andi all those things—if he wanted her to hate him for ever and a day.

'Perhaps if you were to tell me what it is you know about David…?'

Linus gave a rueful shake of his head. 'Oh no, Andi, I'm not stupid enough to give you any more reason to dislike me than you already do.'

Andi could see why he thought that, but she couldn't let him know how she really felt— how she'd been feeling for a while now.

She grimaced. 'I don't understand you half the time, Linus—that is something completely different from dislike.'

He raised his eyes to the ceiling. 'Heaven preserve me from any woman who tries to *understand* me!'

He meant to wound, Andi was sure. And he succeeded. He also succeeded in reminding her that he wasn't a man who had ever committed his emotions to any woman. Just as she wasn't a woman who entered into affairs with a man simply because she wanted him. There was nothing in the least simple about her feelings for Linus.

'And heaven preserve me from a man who's reached the age of almost thirty-seven without even coming close to committing himself to any woman!' she came back, feeling no satisfaction as she saw the ice enter Linus's gaze. 'I'm sorry, Linus.' Andi gave a heavy sigh. 'Can't you see we're just trying to hurt each other? Deliberately. Cruelly.' She gave a sad shake of her head. 'I really don't want to do this.'

Linus could see that by the unhappy curve of her mouth, the pain in the dark depths of her eyes. Damn it, he didn't want to hurt Andi. That was the last thing he wanted to do. He just didn't seem to be able to stop himself…

'You're right.' He nodded abruptly. 'Get some sleep. We have to leave early in the morning if we're going to get to Edinburgh in time for the match.'

Her eyes widened. 'Won't the snow have stopped them from playing?'

'A little bit of snow has never stopped Scotland from playing rugby,' Linus assured her derisively. 'Now, I had better get out of here— before Aunt Mae decides to come and investigate!' he added affectionately before closing the bedroom door softly behind him as he left.

How Andi wished that she and Linus could

at least go back to the easy working relationship they had once had. But today had proved that they never would. That they never could...

CHAPTER NINE

ANDI felt less convinced of that the following afternoon.

By tacit agreement she and Linus had barely spoken on the long drive to Edinburgh after taking early leave of Aunt Mae. The roads had been cleared of snow but the ice still made driving hazardous, requiring Linus to keep his full attention on the road and other traffic. With a brief stop for lunch, they barely made it to Murrayfield in time for the match to start.

Andi was surprised by how much more exciting it was to see the match live; the atmosphere in the huge open-air stadium was electric, the traditional *Flower of Scotland* so emotionally rousing as it was sung by its home crowd that Andi thought she was going to have a problem supporting Wales after all.

Especially when the Scotland team was the

first to score a try, followed by a conversion, throwing the crowded stadium into uproar.

'Still think it's thirty men trying to beat each other to a pulp?' Linus questioned happily as he resumed his seat beside her after standing up to cheer and shout with the rest of the Scotland supporters.

It didn't surprise her that Linus had seats in the midst of the Scotland crowd rather than the more exclusive ones; he might be one of the richest men in Scotland, but, as Mae Harrison had claimed, Linus had never forgotten his roots.

'My grandmother has a more *graphic* description of the game,' Andi returned teasingly.

'If it's the one about it being a game played by men with funny-shaped balls, then I've heard it,' Linus assured her dryly.

Andi found Linus impossible to resist in this boyish mood. 'I'll admit, it's more fun to watch than I thought it would be.'

'I'll make a convert of you yet,' Linus promised as he reached out to take her hand firmly in his before turning his attention back to the game.

Something Andi had trouble doing with her hand held so comfortably in Linus's…

Was Linus aware of what he had just done? Or was it just a completely unconscious gesture on Linus's part, a mutual companionship that actually meant nothing?

Whichever it was, Andi was having trouble concentrating on the game now, relieved when half-time came round and they could stand up, leave their seats and move out with the other fans eager to stretch their legs and discuss the game, although Linus kept a firm hold of her hand so that he didn't lose her in the crowd.

Linus bought them both a hot drink, at last giving Andi the opportunity to release her hand and wrap her fingers about the warming cup.

'So, how do you think it's going?' She attempted conversation.

He grimaced. 'Considering we're twelve-seven down in the first half of the game, not as well as I'd initially hoped. Although you must be pleased,' he added ruefully.

Andi had been too aware of her hand held in Linus's, too aware of Linus himself, to have noticed that the score had changed to Wales's advantage. 'My grandfather will be,' she assured him lightly.

Linus was surprised at how much he was enjoying the match—in spite of the fact that Scotland was losing—in Andi's company. He usually attended these games alone. In fact, he always attended these games alone. He had certainly never thought of bringing a woman with him before, and had only done so because he wanted Andi's opinion on the castle they were going to view tomorrow.

But, strangely, he found Andi's presence at the match quietly companionable rather than irritating, as another woman might have been. He had even, on a couple of occasions, found himself watching Andi's enjoyment of the game rather than watching it himself—something he had never thought would happen when it came to Scotland playing rugby!

He eyed her teasingly. 'Don't tell me you don't find all those muscled thighs exciting?'

Andi raised blonde brows haughtily. 'I've always been more attracted to brains than brawn.'

Of course she had, Linus acknowledged. From what he knew of David Simmington-Browne, the consuming love of Andi's life, he had been a man of suave sophistication. A man who came from the same privileged background as Andi did herself. A man who enjoyed fine dining, the theatre and fast cars. The latter, of course, had been his downfall fifteen months ago when he had crashed his Porsche, killing both himself and Andi's father.

Linus accepted that he was the complete opposite to David Simmington-Browne, and knew that Andi probably thought he lacked any of the other man's polish and sophistication. He had brought Andi to a rugby match, for goodness' sake, instead of taking her to an expensive restaurant.

'Time to go back to our seats,' he announced abruptly as he threw his half-drunk cup of coffee into the nearest bin before striding back to their seats.

Andi frowned at the tense rigidity of Linus's back as she followed him back, aware that he was displeased about something, but having no idea what it was. Perhaps it was just that his beloved Scotland was losing the match?

She didn't hold out much hope of his mood improving, either, when the match ended in Wales's favour.

'I'm sure they'll play better next time,' she attempted encouragingly once they had returned to their vehicle and were driving away from the stadium.

Linus shot her a scathing glance. 'There was nothing wrong with the way they played today, they were just outclassed.'

There didn't seem much Andi could say in

answer to that, so she turned her attention to looking out of the window instead. 'You said that you had made the arrangements for tonight.' They were driving through what looked like a very affluent area, the houses huge, with Mercedes and Jaguars parked in the driveways.

'We're staying at the house of a friend of mine,' Linus answered dismissively.

Andi really wasn't sure she was up to spending another evening in the company of people who were close to Linus. Especially if this friend of Linus's turned out to be as perceptive as Mae Harrison had been.

'He isn't going to be there, Andi,' Linus told her as he sensed her obvious dismay.

Somehow Andi didn't find this information in the least reassuring. 'He isn't?'

'Nope. Keith is in South Africa at the moment, but his housekeeper knows we're stopping by tonight.'

Linus had turned the Range Rover onto what looked to be a private road. The houses here were even more spacious than the previous ones, iron gates at the end of several of the driveways. It was into one of these that Linus turned the vehicle, pressing down the window button so that he could speak into the intercom.

The huge wrought-iron gates opened slowly in front of them.

'This road has been nicknamed Millionaire's Row,' Linus supplied as he saw Andi's eyes widen when they drove down the driveway. They were surrounded by perfectly kept grounds that led up to the long sprawl of a house that Keith affectionately called 'the bungalow'. With over ten *en suite* bedrooms, numerous sitting rooms, an office as well as a study, a long, rambling kitchen deliberately designed with old-fashioned character rather than the more sterile set up Linus had designed for his own apartment at Tarrington Park, the name hardly applied. But, having stayed here numerous times in the past, Linus hadn't given the size or exclusivity of Keith's home another thought until now.

Although after his earlier negative thoughts he couldn't deny that he felt a certain satisfaction at being able to bring Andi to somewhere so exclusive.

Ridiculous, he instantly mocked himself. He was what he was, take it or leave it. That Andi preferred to leave it was her problem, not his.

'Let's go inside where it's warm,' he rasped abruptly once he had parked the Range Rover at the back of the house; he always entered through the kitchen, so why should he consider doing anything differently just because Andi was with him?

The door into the kitchen was open as usual as Linus carried in their bags. The smell of percolated coffee was very inviting, as was the heat being given off by the dark-green Aga across the room; the slate floor was of mellow, yellow stone, the cupboards a dark oak, herbs hanging amongst the gleaming copper pots and pans that hung above the scarred-oak table in the middle of the room.

That Andi liked what she saw, there was no doubt as she looked about her with obvious pleasure. 'Your friend must love to cook.'

Linus's mouth twisted ruefully. 'Keith loves to eat—it's his wife that loves to cook!'

'A perfect combination,' Andi laughed huskily.

'Yes.'

Linus wondered if Andi was as aware of the frisson of awareness between them as he was. The very air seemed stiller. Expectant. As if waiting.

He had stepped over a line with Andi the last few days; now it was time to get their employer-employee relationship back on track. It was either that or they were going to have to part ways…

'I have some papers I need to go through before we look around the castle tomorrow, so feel free to make yourself useful in the kitchen,' he drawled as he opened the door and placed the bags out in the hallway. 'I take it you can cook?' The nature of their relationship meant that Andi's culinary skills, or lack of them, had never come into question before.

'Of course I can cook.'

'Of course you can,' Linus parroted wryly; he should have known his capable PA could do anything she set her mind to.

Andi frowned. 'But I thought the house-keeper opened the gates for us?'

'From the gate house.' Linus nodded, green eyes mocking as he saw Andi's puzzlement. 'Mrs McTaggart doesn't live in, Andi. When Keith is away in South Africa for three months she only acts as caretaker here.' He shrugged. 'I told her we would be fine here on our own, so she's made us coffee as a welcome, and she'll have left some supplies in the fridge for the makings of dinner this evening and breakfast in the morning.'

Andi thought she would rather have had the awkwardness of staying with Linus's friends than finding herself alone with him in this totally private and secluded house in the leafy suburbs of Edinburgh.

She moistened dry lips as she avoided so much as looking at Linus, who stood only feet away from her. 'Perhaps we would be more… comfortable in a hotel?'

'If you mean that *you* would be more comfortable in a hotel, then say so,' Linus shot back. His eyes were narrowed to green, glassy slits, his jaw tight, his mouth thinned with displeasure as Andi looked at him beneath lowered lashes. 'Do you imagine that just because we're alone here I'm going to want to finish what we started the other night?'

'Don't be ridiculous!' Andi felt the warmth in her cheeks. 'I just thought—'

'I'm well aware of what you thought, Andi,' he cut in flatly.

Why—after all the soul-searching, all the warnings Andi had given herself the last forty-eight hours about the danger of revealing her newly realized feelings for Linus—did that assurance actually fill her with disappointment rather than relief?

She turned away. 'I'll see what Mrs McTaggart left for our dinner.'

'Andi?'

She stiffened before turning slowly back to face Linus, her expression guarded. 'Yes?'

Linus hated the way that Andi looked at him now. As if the last year of working so harmoniously together had never happened. As if she no longer trusted him. As if Andi saw him as nothing more than a playboy.

Linus didn't believe that even as a callow youth his actions had been ruled by that particular part of his anatomy. Even in his late teens and early twenties his main driving force had been to succeed. That success hadn't allowed for the emotional baggage of a wife and children, necessitating Linus choosing carefully when it had come to the women he became involved with, with the sole intention that no one got hurt.

Those years of caution had gone completely out of the window the moment he'd kissed Andi three days ago.

'I'm going to use Keith's office.' Linus dismissed her irritably. 'Choose any bedroom you want except the master bedroom; I'll sort something out for myself later.' He strode impatiently from the room before he did or said something he or Andi might regret. He needed space away from Andi to think.

But once he had settled into Keith's spacious office with its view over the back gardens Linus found it difficult to concentrate on the papers he had taken from his briefcase and placed on the desk in front of him. He couldn't get Andi out of his head.

What was he going to do about her? What did he want to do about her?

Those, Linus decided ruefully, were two distinctly different questions.

What he *needed* to do was everything in his power to put their relationship back on the employer-employee basis it had been three days ago.

What he *wanted*, what he ached to do, was strip every piece of clothing from Andi's body before making sweet, intoxicating love to her!

Surprisingly, once alone in the warmth and charm of the rambling kitchen, Andi actually found she was enjoying herself as she took out prawns, steaks, potatoes and a mixture of vegetables from the refrigerator. Along with the selection of herbs strung up amongst the pots and pans in the middle of the kitchen, she had more than enough ingredients to show Linus just how well she could cook.

She even found herself humming happily as she made prawn cocktails, before seasoning the steaks with sea-salt ready for cooking, and then preparing the garlic potatoes and a mélange of fresh vegetables mixed with toasted almonds. She even found the ingredients to prepare a lemon soufflé for dessert as her *pièce de résistance*.

It seemed like years since Andi had actually had the time to enjoy cooking a meal. Her years in London as Gerald Wickham's PA had been busy ones, often requiring her to work long hours, so that she'd only felt like preparing something quick and easy for her dinner once she got home in the evenings. Since Andi had moved back to live in the gate house at Tarrington Park, her mother had initially taken over the cooking, followed by Mrs Ferguson when she'd come to live with them six months ago. Having the use of this wonderful kitchen, and the time in which to prepare what she hoped would be an enjoyable meal, was a complete luxury to Andi.

'I hope that's going to taste as good as it smells!'

Her earlier tension returned at the first sound of Linus's voice as he entered the kitchen almost two hours later. 'I hope so too.' She kept her voice deliberately neutral.

Linus looked at her for several long seconds, looking broodingly handsome in a black sweater with the sleeves pushed up to the elbows and a pair of faded-blue denims that rested low down on his hips. 'Do you think we could call a truce for this evening, Andi?' he finally murmured.

She gave a pained frown. 'I thought we had already tried that.'

'Then maybe we should try harder,' he suggested. 'I don't know about you, but this tension between us is starting to get to me.'

More than get to him, Linus acknowledged ruefully, having done absolutely nothing during the almost-two hours he had sat in Keith's office except stare out of the window as he'd tried to find some sort of solution to the problem between himself and Andi.

He didn't want to lose her as his PA; he had grown to depend on her quiet efficiency this last year.

'I'm no happier about it than you are, Linus,' Andi admitted huskily.

That was something, at least.

'Andi, are you crying?' he prompted disbelievingly as he saw what he thought were tears glistening on her lashes.

Of course she wasn't crying—well, not yet she wasn't, Andi realized as she hastily blinked back the tears she hadn't even known were there until Linus had pointed them out to her—tears of relief that Linus wanted to try to find a way to end this awkwardness between them as much as she did.

'Don't be silly.' She dismissed it. 'I've been peeling onions,' she excused with more brightness than accuracy; she had peeled the onions some time ago, a fact that Linus would realize himself if she gave him too long to think about it. 'I hope you're hungry, because I've prepared a three-course meal for us.'

'Starving!' Linus answered lightly as he took his cue from her. 'Shall I open a bottle of red or white wine to go with it?'

'Your friend doesn't mind you drinking his wine too?' she teased.

Linus shrugged, unconcerned. 'He never has in the past. I'll simply replace it if he does.'

Of course he would. Linus had more than enough money of his own to live in a house like this one if he so chose. Which he didn't. Instead he preferred to spend most of his time in London, with occasional visits to Tarrington Park, and occasional visits to a castle near

Edinburgh if the viewing tomorrow should be a successful one…

Andi grimaced. 'Then strictly speaking we need both, white with the starter and red with the main course, but I'm happy to settle for just red if you are.'

'Whatever the lady wants.' Linus gave an extravagant bow before turning to peruse the wine rack for a suitable bottle of red wine.

Andi stared at the broadness of his back for several long seconds, her heart literally feeling as if it were aching in her chest as she looked at him. She was falling deeper in love with him. She ached to reach out and touch him, to feel the ripple of muscle beneath her fingertips, to put her hands beneath his cashmere sweater and touch the hardness of his chest encased in warm velvet, to touch and caress all of him.

Not the ideal beginning to an evening when they were trying to eliminate all the tension— including sexual—between them.

CHAPTER TEN

'WHAT can I say?' Linus murmured appreciatively as he sat back in his chair at the end of their meal, totally replete with good conversation as well as food. 'You really can cook.' He raised his glass of red wine and toasted Andi across the width of the kitchen table where they had chosen to eat, rather than the formal dining-room further down the hallway.

Her cheeks warmed at his praise. 'I can't say I was exactly pleased with my mother when she insisted I take advanced cookery during my last two years at boarding school.' She smiled affectionately. 'There seemed to be so many more exciting things in life at seventeen and eighteen than learning to cook!'

'Such as?' Linus prompted interestedly, totally at ease after the excellent meal and relaxed conversation.

'Oh, boys, of course.' Andi smiled at the memory.

Linus returned that smile. 'How old were you when you had your first boyfriend?'

'My first boyfriend...?' She frowned, considering. 'Twenty, I think.'

'Twenty!' Linus repeated incredulously, remembering he had been only fourteen when he'd had his first unsuccessful fumbling with a girl in the back row of a cinema.

'I was a very slow starter, okay?' Andi defended herself slightly indignantly. 'Attending an all-girl boarding school didn't help. Again, my mother's idea. She said there would be plenty of time for boys later.'

Except in Andi's case there hadn't been...

By the time she'd started university, she had been almost nineteen, and although she had been taught all the social graces she'd had none of the assurance of her female peers when it had come to flirtation and boys. Oh, she'd been able to converse capably with anyone of any sex and any age, but only in a polite and superficial way. Unfortunately, the boys she had met at university had seen her shyness as cool disinterest rather than the complete lack of experience it really was. Even her first boyfriend had only asked her out because she'd been top of their course and he'd wanted her to help him with his own work. As had the two who'd come after him.

Which was probably one of the reasons Andi had been so ripe for romance and love when David had shown her such a marked interest a year and a half ago...

'It isn't funny, Linus.' She glowered her irritation as she saw his grin.

'I'm not laughing, Andi.' But he continued to smile. 'I'm just trying to imagine you out on your first date at the age of twenty! Where did you go? What did you do?'

Andi glared at Linus. 'We sat in the eating area of a burger takeaway and he asked to look at my notes on *Midsummer Night's Dream*,' she revealed reluctantly.

Linus winced. 'Ooh, *so* not cool!'

'The burger takeaway or the notes?' Surprisingly Andi was starting to enjoy this conversation. It was funny, in retrospect. She simply hadn't thought so at the time. Or felt inclined to repeat those university experiences.

'Both.' Linus gave a disgusted shake of his head.

'I suppose you did something much more so-

phisticated on your first date?' Andi prompted
dryly.

'I was fourteen, and as I recall we went to the
cinema.' He grinned at the memory. 'I chose a
horror movie in the hope that I would have a
chance to take the girl in my arms during the
scary bits.'

'That is so calculating!' Andi laughed huskily
at the vivid image this painted of a very youth-
ful Linus.

'What can I say?' He shrugged. 'I was
fourteen and my hormones had kicked in.'

'And did it work?'

'Not exactly, no,' Linus admitted self-deprecatingly.

He watched Andi through narrowed lids, just
enjoying watching her, liking the way her hips
swayed slightly as she walked, her bottom firm
and round against the material of her denims as
she bent over to begin placing their dirty dishes
in the washer; her sweater fitted snugly against
the pertness of her breasts as she straightened.

He felt his thighs harden in response to that
pert fullness, his pulse starting to race as she bent
over once again. Andi really did have the most
delicious bottom, so curvy and round. So…

'Hey, I should be doing that!' Linus stood up

abruptly as he realized he had been too busy enjoying watching Andi rather than doing any work himself. 'You did the cooking; I don't think you should have to do the clearing away too.' He reached out and took the bowl from Andi's hand, his fingers brushing lightly against her as he did so.

Everything stopped.

Everything.

Time.

Movement.

'Dear God, Andi…!' He groaned harshly as he slammed the bowl down on the side before turning back to take her firmly in his arms, moulding the softness of her curves against his much harder body, knowing by the widening of Andi's eyes as she looked up at him that she felt his arousal pressed against her. 'Don't hate me for this, okay?' he growled huskily. His head lowered and he crushed Andi's lips beneath his, knowing as the feeling of rightness spread through his entire being that this was what he had wanted to do all evening.

To hold Andi. To crush her softness against him. To taste her.

Andi hadn't even seen this coming. She'd been feeling so relaxed after their meal and the light conversation, relieved that they were actually talking comfortably together again, that the fierceness of Linus's desire totally took her by surprise.

And thrilled her.

There was no way that she could deny the warm surge of her own desire as Linus's lips devoured hers. He pressed her even closer to that pulsing hardness of his thighs, and ignited a burning response deep inside her as the kiss deepened and lengthened.

It was as if they had both been waiting for this moment. As if everything else that had happened the last twenty-four hours was irrelevant. Their passion felt as intense as it had been the previous evening, totally consuming, brooking no denial.

Andi's arms moved up to Linus's shoulders and her fingers became entangled in the dark thickness of the hair at his nape as she held nothing back from her response. Lips parted. Tongues duelled. Their breath hot and heavy. Laboured. Linus's hands roamed wildly down her back, her hips, before cupping her bottom to hold her against him as his hardened thighs thrust into hers with the same rhythm as his tongue claimed and thrust into the moist cavern of her mouth.

Her back arched as Linus's mouth left hers to trail a path of heat down the length of her throat. Licking. Tasting. Biting. Sending her totally out of control. Her nipples were highly sensitized, her inner thighs on fire. Hot. Moist. Aching.

She offered no resistance as Linus lifted her sweater and pulled it totally over her head, baring her breasts to his heated gaze.

Linus had never seen Andi looking so wild and unkempt. Her hair was a golden tangle about her naked shoulders where he had pulled the sweater over her head before discarding it. Her eyes were almost black, her mouth red and pouting, lips slightly parted.

'You are so beautiful!' Linus murmured appreciatively as the heat of his gaze fixed on the swollen softness of her breasts with their aroused and inviting, dusky-rose tips.

He lifted his hands to cup each of those creamy breasts, feeling their weight in his palms as he ran the pad of his thumbs across the already roused nipples, his gaze moving quickly back to Andi's face as she gave a low, throaty groan in response to that caress.

Her lids were slightly lowered over glittering, dark eyes, her throat arched, lips parted, the tip of her tongue moving moistly across those parted lips as if she could still taste him there.

His thumbs caressed her again, thighs pulsing anew as Andi arched into that caress and her hands moved up to curve her fingers about his wrists. Inviting. Begging. Pleading— for more.

Linus gave her more, claiming her mouth once again even as he continued to caress the tips of her ultra-sensitive breasts.

Andi moaned low in her throat as Linus took her nipples between his thumb and finger and rolled them lightly, then harder, pressing, pinching; Andi's groans became breathless gasps, her inner thighs on fire.

The pleasure of Linus's caresses was overwhelming; mindless pleasure. Only the demands of her body were important. And her body demanded Linus—all of him.

She wrenched her mouth from Linus's, his skin feeling hot and slightly damp as her fingers brushed lightly against him. She reached down to pull his sweater up his body and over his head, before throwing it to the floor beside her own.

Andi moved instinctively as she touched his bared flesh, her skin very pale against his as her fingers tangled in the dark hair that grew across his chest and then down in a vee beneath his denims.

Linus was just as broad-shouldered and beautifully male as Andi had imagined he would be; his skin was slightly salty-tasting as she kissed him. Kissed his shoulders. The hollow at the base of his throat. His chest. The tight buds nestled amongst the dark hair.

His chest moved against her as Linus groaned huskily, and one of his hands became entangled in the length of her hair, bunching those tresses in his clenched fist as she flicked her tongue lightly over that hardened nub.

Once again Linus lost his breath, all of his senses concentrated on the ministrations of Andi's lips and tongue as she pleasured him in a way no other woman ever had. Linus experienced pleasure he had never known before, a pleasure that shot straight to his groin and down the length of his legs.

He had always been the lover. The instigator. The one in control.

Andi had wrenched that away from him the moment she'd begun to touch him. To kiss him.

She had turned the attentions of her mouth to his other nipple now, and her hands moved caressingly down the side of his waist and then to the length of his back, fingers lightly caressing, nails slightly rasping. Sending quivers of pleasure down the length of his spine.

His buttocks tensed, thighs instantly thrusting, his arousal throbbing demandingly.

He wanted Andi. Now!

But they had too many clothes on still.

Both of them!

Linus moved back slightly. 'I'm not going anywhere,' he assured her gruffly as Andi looked up at him protestingly for stopping her own pleasure. His gaze continued to hold hers as his hands moved to the fastening of her denims, unzipping them to pull them over the curve of her hips and down the length of her legs, before slipping her feet from them one at a time.

'I've always wondered how, in circumstances like these, people undressed with any degree of dignity,' she murmured softly. 'Now I see that dignity is of no consequence whatsoever at times like these,' she added with light self-mockery.

Linus barely heard her, his attention fixed on Andi's last article of clothing. A pair of cream silk-and-lace briefs was now the only thing between him and the hot centre of her arousal that he had caressed only once and desperately wanted to touch again.

The scrap of silk and lace ripped easily in his hand, baring Andi completely, her gasp of surprise quickly followed by another as Linus lifted her and sat her on top of the wooden table before parting her thighs to his avid gaze.

She was as beautiful as Linus had known she would be. Her curls were a slightly darker blonde than her hair, the petals of her inner thighs open and the same dusky-rose colour as her nipples.

He touched her there, feeling how hot she was.

Linus groaned softly as he moved down onto his knees, parting Andi's thighs even further before his hands moved to caress her.

Andi totally lost control the moment Linus's tongue rasped against her before thrusting deep inside her, feeling her own release as wave after wave of pleasure surged through every particle of her, from her head down to her toes. Linus continued that rhythmic thrust inside her until he had drained every last, quivering, shudder-ing moment from her.

Andi put her hands down on the table behind her to stop herself from falling as she collapsed back weakly, eyes closed, her body continuing to quiver and shake.

Finally she raised sleepy lids to look at

him, the darkness of his hair wild on his shoulders, his eyes a deep, dark green as he looked up at her, a sensual curve to his sculptured lips.

Andi had no idea why she should suddenly feel so shy—after all, Linus already knew her body more intimately than any other person ever had.

'Sorry.' Linus grimaced as he saw her hesitation, instead standing up to step between her parted thighs. 'Too much too soon,' he accepted ruefully as a hand curved gently against one of her heated cheeks.

'No.' She shook her head. 'No,' she assured him again huskily as she reached out tentatively to touch his chest, instantly feeling the hard throb of his heartbeat. The same throb as his arousal.

Her gaze held his as that hand moved down to unfasten his own denims, sliding down the zip to run her fingers lightly, caressingly, against the hardness of his shaft. Instantly she felt it surge, its need to break free.

Andi slid lightly off the table as she slowly peeled those denims down his hips and thighs, taking his briefs with them and discarding both, before her hand moved and her fingers curled about the thick length of Linus's arousal. She heard his sharply indrawn breath before he leant back against the table, hands gripping the edge either side of him.

Andi watched Linus's face as she began to move her hand slowly up and down. His ragged breathing, the slight flush to his cheeks, told her how much he was enjoying the caress. Her fingers tightened slightly as she felt the hot pulse of blood beneath her hand, her thumb moving to caress the red tip, feeling the escape of moisture there.

'Lie back, Linus,' she encouraged huskily.

His gaze didn't leave hers as he swept the remains of their meal to one end of the table before lowering himself back, arousal jutting temptingly, hands clenching at his sides, as Andi began a trail of kisses, starting at his chest and slowly moving lower.

Linus hissed in a sharp breath, eyes closing, jaw clenching as he felt the heat of Andi's mouth close about him, the slow rasp of her tongue instantly driving him wild. He was too aroused to be able to take much more of this.

He grasped her shoulders, reluctantly drawing her away from him as he lifted her up onto his chest. 'I want to be inside you, Andi,' he grated fiercely as he moved her so that, by straddling his waist, she brought her heat against his arousal.

Andi wanted that too, wanted Linus buried deep, deep inside her. So deep inside her that she wouldn't know where she ended and Linus began!

'Not yet!' Her hands rested on his shoulders as she kissed and licked his chest.

His head surged up from the table top as he took fierce possession of her nipple, drawing it deeply into the heat of his mouth as he began to suckle, his hand cupping her other breast as his thumb caressed her.

Andi's second climax of the evening was even more intense than her first, the pleasure intense, seemingly never-ending, becoming even more so as Linus surged inside her.

Then, a brief moment, a mere second, of pain as he pierced the barrier of her virginity, that pain quickly replaced with aching satisfaction.

He raised his head, his face dark. 'Andi?'

'Not now, Linus,' she repeated, aching, and for quite a different reason. Her expression was fierce, her hair wild about her shoulders as she looked down at him.

'But—'

'No, Linus!' She didn't want a discussion now. Didn't want to talk about why she was still a virgin at the age of nearly twenty-eight.

Andi held his gaze as she began to move, slowly at first, wary of that earlier pain. But there was no pain now, only those long, deep strokes of Linus's body inside hers. Strokes that made Linus forget all his questions, or her answers, as he tightly gripped her hips to match her rhythm as he moved up and into her to give them both the maximum pleasure.

It was wonderful. Linus was wonderful. More wonderful than Andi could ever have imagined, and Linus was with her totally as she rode the crest of her next climax, until she collapsed weakly against his chest, only the sound of their ragged breathing disturbing the utter peace of the moment.

Andi was filled with that inner peace. A deep, satisfying peace.

Like the calm in the eye of the storm.

It couldn't last, of course; Linus had questions. And once he was recovered Linus was going to demand that Andi give him answers to those questions.

But for the moment—this brief, peaceful, ecstatic moment in time—Andi felt completely and utterly happy.

CHAPTER ELEVEN

'ANDI, what the hell just happened?' Linus scowled darkly.

She gave him a rueful glance. 'I'm sure you know that better than I do.'

They had dressed in silence once they had gone through the awkwardness of separating and removing themselves from the kitchen table.

He had made love to Andi on top of a table; Linus inwardly winced. Keith and Lindsay's kitchen table. Linus would never be able to visit here again without remembering that!

'I was your first lover,' he rasped, still totally incredulous at that fact. In awe, if he was honest. As far as he was aware, he had never been any woman's 'first' before. That it should be Andi, of all women, had thrown him totally.

Andi's met his gaze steadily. 'I know that.'

'*I* didn't.' Impatience crept into his tone.

She shrugged. 'Does it matter?'

'Well, of course it—' Linus broke off, breathing deeply. 'I thought—I had assumed that you and Simmington-Browne were lovers.'

Andi stiffened. 'Then you assumed wrong.'

'I'm not in the mood for your ice-maiden tactics at the moment, Andi,' he warned impatiently, a nerve pulsing erratically in his tightly clenched jaw.

She eyed him sternly. 'Couldn't we talk about this in the morning, Linus?'

'No, we can't talk about it in the morning!' he bit back harshly.

No, they really couldn't, Andi acknowledged heavily. Which was a pity. Because she already knew from the darkness of Linus's mood that all of the pleasure that had gone before, the closeness she had felt with him as they'd made love together, was going to be completely obliterated by the dangerous anger she could now feel glowering beneath the surface. Linus stood across the room, staring at her with brooding eyes.

She sighed deeply. 'Most men would just feel flattered to have been a woman's first lover.'

His mouth tightened; his eyes were a glacial green. 'I'm not *most men*.'

No, he certainly wasn't. Linus was the man she loved. Even more so now, Andi acknowledged heavily. Just as she knew that what he felt towards her was anger and a certain amount of resentment. 'Stop making such a big deal out of it, Linus.'

'It is a big deal, damn it!' he rasped fiercely, hands clenched at his sides. 'I had no idea. I would never have allowed it to go that far between us if…' He shook his head, knowing he would have been gentler with her if he had known, more—more what? Linus veered away from answering any questions about his own emotions. 'What were you thinking of, allowing things to get so out of control when you've obviously never been with a man before?'

Andi hadn't been thinking at all. Deliberately so. She had just enjoyed the moment. The joy of being made love to by Linus.

But obviously he wasn't prepared to let that lack of conscious thought continue. Just as Andi wasn't prepared to totally humiliate herself by allowing Linus to see her true feelings for him.

She gave a dismissive shrug. 'Maybe our time together the other night showed me that I'm tired of being a twenty-seven-year-old virgin. Maybe I was curious to know what came next.'

'You aren't that naïve, Andi,' Linus retorted scornfully. 'It's pretty obvious from what happened just now that you knew *exactly* what came next!'

She eyed him curiously. 'Can I take it from that remark that you didn't find me disappointing as a lover?'

Disappointing? That was the last way that Linus would have described Andi as a lover. Mind blowing. A sensual delight. Sheer, unadulterated pleasure. But disappointing? No!

He felt that nerve pulsing in his tightly clenched jaw. 'You were curious to know what came next, Andi?' He latched on to her earlier statement. 'Does that mean I was some sort of experiment, to see what you've been missing all these years?'

She gave a pained frown. 'I'm not sure I would have put it quite like that.'

'Then how would you have put it? Damn it, Andi!' Linus turned away impatiently, as angry with himself as he was with her.

He should have known, should have guessed from Andi's comment about people undressing 'in these circumstances', that something wasn't quite as it seemed. But he had been too lost in his own arousal at the time. He had wanted Andi too much to genuinely take in the meaning of what she had said. Besides, even completely compos mentis, he doubted he would ever have guessed that Andi was still a virgin.

It had just never occurred to him. Why should it? Andi had been involved with David Simmington-Browne for a couple of months before his death. She had been engaged to marry the man!

There was also the fact that Linus couldn't imagine any man looking at Andi and not wanting her...

Even now—confused, angry; sheer, bloody furious, if he was honest—Linus knew he still wanted her.

Which had absolutely no bearing whatsoever on their present situation. In fact, it only served to confuse the issue.

'What are we supposed to do now, Andi?' he prompted bleakly.

She shook her head. 'Let's not complicate things, Linus.'

'No?' His mouth twisted.

'No!'

'So you're suggesting we just go to bed—separately—and then tomorrow morning it's business as usual?'

When he put it like that...

Andi's chin rose defensively. 'Would you rather I just left quietly now?'

Linus gave a derisive shake of his head. 'I
doubt there would be any trains home this time
of the night. Or that any of the local hotels have
a room available, following the match this afternoon.' He ran a hand impatiently through his
already dishevelled hair. 'No, Andi, I'm afraid
you're stuck with me for tonight at least.'

Considering Andi would have liked nothing
better than to be 'stuck with' him for the rest of
her life, a single night spent under the same
roof as Linus didn't seem like such a hardship.

But that wasn't what Linus meant, was it?

Andi moistened suddenly dry lips. 'What do
you want to do about this situation, Linus?'

'I have no idea,' he bit out bleakly.

She nodded ruefully. 'Besides wishing that it
had never happened, of course.'

His eyes were narrowed to icy-green slits.
'It's a little late for that, isn't it?'

Far, far too late, Andi realized. She had made
a mistake. A big one. And it was a mistake that
she now realized was going to cost her dearly.

Linus sighed. 'I guess we have two options
open to us.'

By the grimness of Linus's expression,
options Andi was already sure that she wasn't
going to like!

'Option one,' he continued flatly. 'You leave my employment immediately we return to Tarrington Park.'

'With suitable references as regards my work, I hope?' Andi's mouth had gone dry.

A nerve pulsed in Linus's clenched jaw as he nodded. 'You really *are* the best damned PA in the western hemisphere.'

Andi gave a humourless smile. 'Thank you.'

'You're welcome,' Linus drawled. 'Option two is for the two of us to continue with this relationship as is for as long as it's agreeable to both of us.'

Andi stared at him disbelievingly, not sure she had heard him correctly. Was Linus really suggesting she either leave his employment or they continue sleeping together?

But what other alternatives did they have? They certainly couldn't continue working together as if this evening had never happened. Andi certainly couldn't, at least.

Which, she now accepted, had been her mistake.

She hadn't thought, hadn't wanted to think, beyond making love with Linus; had longed for it so much that when the opportunity had presented itself she'd simply not been able to resist. Effectively ending her employment with Linus, or entering into an affair with him—these were the options, it seemed.

'"As is"?' she repeated slowly. 'You're proposing that we continue going to bed together as well as working together until one or both of us tires of the arrangement?'

The panic rose in Andi's chest even as she repeated Linus's suggestion. Could she live with that? Could she become Linus's mistress until he tired of her? The alternative—never to see Linus again once she and her mother had left the gate house at Tarrington Park—was even less acceptable to her.

'It's an idea,' she acknowledged shakily.

Linus's mouth thinned. 'Do I take it from that you didn't find me too disappointing as a lover?' he taunted, at once feeling an absolute bastard as he saw the colour first enter and then drain from Andi cheeks.

'And if I didn't?' Her stance was challenging now.

Linus grimaced. 'I would say you have no other experience with which to compare my performance.'

Andi drew in a sharp breath. 'I really don't think that is any of your business.'

'Why weren't you and Simmington-Browne lovers?' he cut in impatiently. 'The two of you were engaged, were going to be married.'

'Maybe, between the demands of David's career and my own, we just didn't find the time,' she evaded.

Andi had thought long and hard about her relationship with David the last few days, and realized there had been a definite lack of inclination to make love to her on David's part. A reluctance that made Andi question her own sexual appeal until Linus had made love to her, she now realized.

It had also made her question why it was she had been content to leave their relationship as it was until after she and David were married.

David had been everything Andi could have wished for in her future husband: handsome, suave, wealthy. She had enjoyed being with him, had looked forward to becoming his wife. But, at the same time, she had been quite content to wait for a physical relationship between them, as had David.

Linus's response to her just now had told Andi only too clearly that the other man's reluctance wasn't because she lacked sexual allure, after all.

Now she couldn't help wondering if the reason for David's reluctance didn't have something to do with the hints Linus had made over the last few days that she hadn't really known him at all...

'I would have made the time and opportunity,' Linus rasped.

'You aren't David—' Andi broke off abruptly as she realized how accusatory she had sounded by the sudden tensing of Linus's expression. 'What I meant to say was—'

'I know what you meant, Andi,' Linus bit out. 'Obviously you consider it's absolutely fine for me to initiate you into physical pleasure while the saintly David remains firmly on top of his pedestal!' He was too angry now to even care how stricken Andi looked suddenly, her face pale.

'Linus, please don't.'

'Don't what?' he challenged harshly. 'Don't ruin all your infatuated memories of the man?' He shook his head. 'He had feet of clay, Andi. He was a fake. A liar. He was responsible for—' Linus broke off abruptly, drawing in a deep, controlling breath as he realized exactly what he was doing: exactly what he had promised himself he wouldn't do.

It was past time Andi knew the truth about the

man she had been going to marry. She deserved to know, *had* to know, if she was ever going to move on with her life.

But not from him, Linus realized.

Never from him.

He ran an agitated hand through the dark thickness of his hair. 'For the moment, I think it better if we go for an as-yet unmentioned third option—which is that we don't make any rash decisions this evening. Well, anything more rash than we've already done,' he added in disgust.

Andi's breath left her in a shaky sigh, her first indication that she had even been holding it in. Several times over the last few days Linus had seemed on the brink of telling her something about David. Something she hadn't known...

Something she still didn't know.

'If you have something to say about David, then I really wish you would just say it.'

'So that you can hate me more than you already do?' Linus taunted. He gave a derisive shake of his head. 'I think not, Andi.'

'Do you think you're being fair, Linus?' She glared darkly.

'At the moment I can't even think straight enough to answer that question intelligently,' he acknowledged disdainfully. 'You want answers, Andi? I'm sorry—' he shook his head '—but you aren't going to get them from me.' He gave a rueful grimace.

'Who, then?'

He drew in a long, shuddering breath. 'Maybe you should try asking someone a little closer to home.'

Andi frowned, totally at a loss as to who he could mean. Loving Linus as she did, he was the closest person to her that she knew... 'My mother?' she gasped disbelievingly.

Linus at once regretted that his frustration with this situation had led to his revealing that Marjorie was as aware of David Simmington-Browne's shortcomings as he was. Just as Linus knew that it had been Marjorie's decision not to reveal those shortcomings to her already-heartbroken daughter that had actually contributed to her own breakdown of emotions just over a year ago.

It was something Marjorie definitely didn't want her daughter to know, as Linus knew from long conversations with the older woman on the afternoons they had sat drinking tea together.

'Linus?'

He scowled his frustration with this situation. 'Let's just forget we ever had this conversation, hmm? Why the hell should I care if you go on thinking of Simmington-Browne as some sort of untarnished god?'

Why indeed? Linus wondered dully.

'Look, we'll get the viewing of the castle over early tomorrow morning and then start our journey back immediately afterwards.' He spoke briskly. 'Maybe we can both get a little perspective on this situation once we're back at Tarrington Park,' he added.

Andi eyed him frustratedly, more than ever determined to find out the truth that Linus was choosing to keep from her—that he had no right to keep from her. That Andi had no intention of remaining in ignorance of for a moment longer than she had to.

'Leave that,' Linus rasped as she turned to begin clearing away their dinner things. 'You did the cooking; I'll tidy all this away before I go to bed.'

Andi didn't even bother to argue with the offer, instead turning and quietly leaving the kitchen to go to the bedroom she was to use for the night.

She had to.

Before she broke down and cried. The sight of the dinner things in such disarray reminded her all too forcefully of how she and Linus had made such wild, exciting love there only minutes earlier.

CHAPTER TWELVE

'YOU'RE sure this is what you want?' Linus's expression was grim as he spoke through the door of the carriage, where Andi now stood as she waited for the train to pull out of Edinburgh station.

On its way to London. Where Andi would then board another train that would take her back to the village of Tarrington, and then home.

Andi had been pale and withdrawn when she'd emerged from her bedroom this morning, refusing all offers of breakfast before informing him that she had decided to go home on the first available train. Linus had tried to talk her out of it, of course—even repeating the excuse that he needed her advice on the castle he was to view this morning—but Andi had remained adamant in her decision. In the circumstances, Linus had had no choice but to drive her to the railway station.

Quite what else Andi had decided during the long night-hours Linus had yet to hear.

For the moment it was enough that Andi was leaving. 'I thought we were going to have another talk this morning?' he prompted softly.

She gave a shake of her head. Her hair was a golden curtain about her shoulders, her eyes huge and dark in the pallor of her face. 'I think what we both need at the moment is to put some distance between us. At least for a few days.' She repeated the same argument she had made earlier for leaving this morning.

What Andi really meant, Linus felt sure, was that she needed to put some distance between herself and him.

He gave a snort of frustration. 'How can I make a decision on this castle without your input on the place?'

She gave a humourless smile. 'The same way you made decisions before I came to work for you a year ago.'

He didn't want to go back to the way he had made decisions before Andi had begun working for him. He didn't want to go back to his lonely way of life before Andi had come into it at all!

'I thought we were a team.' He scowled, aware that his argument lacked conviction, but unable for the moment to do anything about it. Andi was leaving. And he had no way of stopping that from happening.

Andi's smile became rueful. 'I'm an employee, Linus, not part of a team.' And Andi had decided that even *that* had to end once Linus returned to Tarrington Park. There was no way she could continue working for him. Not now. Not when they had become lovers.

It was a decision, a hard battle of a decision, that Andi had come to during the long, wakeful hours of the night. Much as she hated the idea of leaving him, dreaded it, Andi knew she wouldn't be able to continue working for Linus after last night. Even if they could somehow try to continue working together, Andi knew she could no longer bear even the thought of the numerous women she would witness going in and out of Linus's life—those weeks when Linus would disappear up to London to spend most of his nights with the latest woman to share his bed.

She was a fool for falling in love with him, for ever allowing things to get so out of control between them, but she certainly wasn't a masochist.

'You're part of *my* team, Andi.' Linus was frowning as he reached out to cover her hand with his as it rested on top of the lowered window. 'Don't make any decisions until I come back, hmm?' he encouraged huskily as the guard on the platform whistled that the train was about to leave.

Andi's expression was one of deep sadness. 'We both know what my decision has to be, Linus.'

'No, it doesn't!' he rasped impatiently as the guard gave another whistle before stepping onto the train. 'Promise me that you won't do anything until I get back?'

She raised blonde brows. 'Do anything, Linus?' Her mouth twisted derisively. 'What do you imagine I'm going to do—take another couple of lovers as soon as I get home so that I do have something with which to compare your own performance?'

Linus's eyes narrowed even as his hand tightened painfully on hers. 'Don't even think about it!'

Her eyes widened. 'Aren't you being a little dictatorial, even for you?'

Even for him...

Is that what Andi really thought of him—that he was some sort of dictator, who insisted his instructions be obeyed?

Admittedly in the past Linus had been pretty singleminded. He had always known what he wanted and where he was going. But after last night he had no idea what happened next. Except that he wasn't willing to let Andi just walk out of his life...

Her smile was pained. 'Goodbye, Linus,' she murmured huskily as the train began to pull out of the station.

Goodbye?

No way was this goodbye. Absolutely no way!

Linus began to walk along by the side of the train. 'I want your promise that you will still be at Tarrington Park when I get back.' He shouldn't have agreed to Andi going home on the train at all. Should have insisted on driving her there. Who cared about some castle in the middle of Scotland, anyway?

'You have to let go, Linus!' Andi told him. His long strides were no longer enough as the train began to pick up speed, the end of the platform finally forcing him to release her hand. Andi moved forward to look back at him out of the window—a solitary, somehow lonely figure standing at the end of the platform, hands thrust into the pockets of his overcoat, expression grim as he called out to her. 'I can't hear you,' she answered as those parting words were carried away on the icy breeze. Her last vision of Linus became blurred as the tears she had been holding back for so long refused to be denied any longer.

She stumbled to a seat at the back of the carriage, relieved there was no one sitting beside her to witness her tears, hot, silent tears that refused to stop. Andi was totally blind to the beauty of the snow-covered landscape outside the window as the train sped quickly on its way to London. Bringing her ever closer to Tarrington Park, and a conversation with her mother concerning David that appeared to be long overdue.

That Linus regretted even telling her that much, Andi didn't doubt, having seen the regret on his face the moment he'd spoken. Too late, of course. Andi had every intention now of talking to her mother about David. Of learning exactly what it was that Linus and her mother knew about him that she didn't…

'You look exhausted, darling.' Her mother greeted her as Andi let herself in the back door of the gate house very late that evening.

So late that Andi was surprised her mother

was still up. The kitchen was far from her mother's favourite domain, either... 'You've spoken to Linus,' she guessed easily as she put her bag down on the kitchen table.

Her mother gave a rueful smile. 'He thought it best that I know you were on your way home.'

'I'll make a pot of coffee, darling, and then we can talk, if that's what you want?' Her mother looked at her questioningly.

Andi's resolve stiffened. 'It is.' She was exhausted, from the tears she had cried as much as from the long train journey, but not too exhausted to talk to her mother.

Marjorie nodded before moving to prepare the coffee. Andi sat down at the kitchen table. For the first time in a very long time, it seemed, she took a good look at her mother. The trauma Marjorie had suffered at Miles's death fifteen months ago had faded, and at fifty-eight she was still a beautiful woman. Her hair and make-up were always perfect, her figure still trim and shapely.

Andi also knew that her mother's social life had picked up in the last six months, that Marjorie now attended a weekly bridge-club at the house of one of her friends in the next village. The social connection had led to other invitations: to coffee mornings with her female friends, the occasional game of golf at the local golf club, and several parties over the Christmas period.

Yes, her mother was much more together now than she had been a year ago when Andi had moved from London to live and work at Tarrington Park. Together enough to face the possibility of moving once again? Andi hoped so…

Marjorie placed a cup of coffee in front of Andi before sitting across the kitchen table from her, the two of them drinking in companionable silence for several minutes before she spoke. 'Linus told me that you have concerns about David.'

Concerns? Andi had so many questions about him, she didn't quite know where to start!

She gave a shaky sigh. 'Why was it, do you suppose, when he so obviously wasn't in love with me, that David asked me to marry him?'

Her mother looked taken aback. 'But of course he loved you, darling!'

'No.' Andi was emphatic in her denial. She had thought about David long and hard on the journey back from Scotland, and the question she'd kept coming back to was the one that Linus had asked last night: if David had been in love with her, then why hadn't he made any effort to *make* love to her? The answer to that now seemed all too obvious—because David hadn't been in love with her. And if he hadn't been in love with her, then there had to be another reason why he had asked her to marry him. 'No, he didn't,' she repeated firmly, her gaze steadily meeting her mother's.

Marjorie looked startled. 'Oh, but I always thought—I always believed—that loving you was David's one redeeming quality!' She frowned.

'And his *unredeeming* qualities?' Andi prompted sadly.

Marjorie gave a shuddering sigh. 'He was dishonest. A thief. Totally responsible for ruining your father—no; perhaps that's being a little unfair.' She gave a pained sigh.

Andi gave shaky laugh. 'But only *a little*?'

Her mother nodded. 'He wasn't totally responsible; your father simply trusted him too much. Even more so once you and David became engaged. After all, David was going to become his son-in-law.'

Andi had already realized in the last few days that she hadn't been in love with David at all, that she had been more in love with the idea of being in love than with David himself. That she had been swept off her feet by the attentions of such a handsome and sophisticated man. And she had also come to realize that she hadn't really known David.

From the little Linus had implied, and the things her mother had already said, it would seem that Andi had known David even less than she had thought!

'What did he do to Daddy?' she prompted softly, reaching out to clasp her mother's hand with her own as she saw the way it trembled on the table top.

Marjorie shook her head. 'Oh, their first business-venture together was genuine enough. Your father made thousands of pounds out of it,' she added affectionately. 'But that initial success was only the lure, to encourage your father to invest more and more money. After that first success, there was one bogus business-deal after another, the money your father invested going straight into David's own bank-account—'

'But why?' Andi gasped disbelievingly. 'David was rich.'

'But he wasn't, darling.' Her mother's hand gripped hers. 'It was all just a façade. Another lie,' she admitted shakily. 'His car was rented. His apartment in London too. Everything David ever told us about himself was a lie.' Marjorie shook her head. 'Oh, his family had been wealthy at one time, but apparently his father lost it all in one speculation after another while David was still at school. He— Apparently David decided once he was an adult that he was going to get it all back, by fair means or foul. Your father was far from the first person he had duped in that way.' Tears glistened on Marjorie's lashes.

Andi was totally shaken; her mother's revelations were so much worse than she had even imagined during her long journey from Scotland. Andi felt sick just at the thought of Linus possibly knowing those things about the man she had thought she loved. The man she had been going to marry...

She swallowed hard. 'Why did David ask me to marry him?'

Her mother's hand gripped hers tightly now. 'I think—I've come to believe—it may have been because he realized your father had slowly been coming to an awareness of what was going on. That David knew your father was going to confront him with it. That David felt there would be less chance of your father causing a scandal if he were engaged to marry his daughter.'

Andi closed her eyes, feeling dizzy as well as sick. It all made so much sense to her now. All of it. 'Why didn't you tell me?' she choked, tears in her own eyes as she looked across at her mother. 'Why didn't you try to stop me from becoming engaged to him? Why didn't Daddy?'

'He would *never* have let you marry David, darling, if what he'd suspected turned out to be true,' Marjorie assured her vehemently. 'But you seemed so happy, so much in love—and your father wanted to talk to David first before we said anything to you. To make absolutely sure that David really was guilty of the things we suspected before we broke your heart.'

Andi became very still as a sudden thought struck her with the force of a blow. 'The day of the accident—that was the day Daddy had decided to confront David, wasn't it…?'

'Yes.' The tears fell unchecked down Marjorie's cheeks.

Andi couldn't think, could barely breathe. 'Do you think it was really an accident at all? Or do you think—?'

'We have to believe—the coroner ruled it as such,' her mother stated firmly, as if the alternative was still too awful to contemplate.

'Believe me, Andi, it does no good to dwell on it, to imagine it being otherwise. It can't bring your father back. Or David.'

'If what we suspect is true, then he wouldn't deserve to be brought back!' Andi bit out fiercely. 'He ruined Daddy. May even be responsible, intentionally or accidentally, for Daddy's death!'

'We don't know that for sure, darling,' her mother soothed.

Andi didn't need to know for sure. That David was guilty of all those other things was enough to totally erase the guilt Andi had been feeling over the last few days at the realization that she had never loved David at all. That she had simply been overwhelmed, flattered, by the attentions of such a charming and successful man.

It had all been a sham. A lie.

All of it.

She felt angry on her father's behalf, sorrow on her mother's—but for herself she knew this knowledge gave her a sense of freedom. Of liberation. From that lingering loyalty to a man who had no more been in love with her than Andi had been in love with him. She understood that now.

She hadn't even known what love was eighteen months ago.

What she felt for Linus was love, of the deepest kind. She not only loved the way he looked, she also loved the man that he was—the man that he had become despite, or because of, his tough upbringing. He was a man who had never forgot or denied his roots, or the two women—his mother and Aunt Mae—who had brought him up against all the odds to be honest and hard-working.

Linus was the exact opposite of David. Linus was a man who had been just as determined to turn his fortune around, but legitimately, honestly, and through sheer, hard work and gritty determination. Linus didn't use people to achieve his goals. He didn't lie to them. What and who he was was there for everyone to see, and people could either like him or loathe him for it.

Andi loved him for it.

She turned back to her mother, smiling reassuringly as she saw the anxious look on Marjorie's face. 'It's okay. *I'm* okay.' She squeezed her mother's hand. 'Linus knows all of this too, doesn't he?' she prompted.

Her mother sighed deeply. 'He…guessed at first, I think. He realized that your father's bankruptcy, the debts, just didn't add up.' She shook her head. 'He came and had tea with me the day he found out the truth. He's a good man, Andi. An astute man.'

Not astute enough, thank goodness, to realize that Andi was in love with him!

'Why didn't you tell me the truth about David after the accident?' She frowned her puzzlement.

Marjorie shook her head. 'You were so upset. So devastated. I— It just didn't seem right to burden you with anything else. Your father was dead. David was dead. Nothing I did or said after the fact was going to change that.'

'So instead you made yourself ill carrying that particular burden alone?' Andi realized heavily.

Her mother's smile was tearful. 'Didn't you already have enough to cope with? As well as losing your father and David, you had to change your job in order to move here and be with me.' She shook her head. 'I decided, rightly or wrongly, that it was better to just leave things as they were. That you would forget about David in time and move on. Have you moved on, Andi?' Her mother looked at her expectantly.

Andi's expression became guarded. 'Perhaps,' she admitted reluctantly. 'For all the good it's going to do me!' she added forcefully.

'What do you mean?'

Andi gave a shaky laugh. 'As soon as Linus gets back here, I intend handing in my resignation.'

'But why?' her mother gasped.

Andi couldn't quite meet her mother's gaze now. 'I— It's a little complicated.' Marjorie wasn't as easily shocked as she had once been, but nevertheless there were certain things one simply did not confide in one's mother.

'In what way? What do you mean, when Linus gets back?' her mother pressed.

'He's still in Scotland.'

'No, he isn't.' Her mother shook her head. 'Linus came to see me an hour or so ago, Andi, shortly after he got back.'

'But—'

'Linus is at Tarrington Park,' her mother stated clearly, so that there should be absolutely no misunderstanding as to her meaning.

Andi stood up abruptly to go over to the kitchen window and look out across the parkland towards Tarrington Park. Sure enough, the lights in Linus's apartment at the top of the house were all ablaze—and, unless Andi's eyes deceived her, a lone figure stood at one of the windows looking straight back at her…

CHAPTER THIRTEEN

'Good morning, Andi,' Linus greeted her cautiously as he entered her office the morning following his return to Tarrington Park, knowing that Andi would have spoken to her mother on her own return the previous evening, and unsure what her mood was going to be.

She looked normal enough in one of her smart business-suits and pristine-white blouses.

Andi looked up from the post she had been going through when he'd come in. 'I didn't expect you back from Scotland until tomorrow.'

'No, well, change of plan.' He shrugged impatiently. 'How was your journey yesterday?'

'Fine, thanks. Yours?'

Damn it, they would be discussing the weather next! 'Fine, thanks,' he dismissed lightly. 'I called in briefly to see Jim and Jennie on the way back—took Jennie some flowers and Jim a box of cigars, to thank them for their hospitality.'

Andi gave a cool inclination of her head. 'That was nice of you.'

Linus's mouth tightened. 'I can be nice, Andi.'

'I've never claimed otherwise.' She returned his gaze coolly.

To think that Linus had once cultivated, even appreciated, this coolness of Andi's. Now it just made him want to shake her until her teeth rattled.

He grimaced. 'You've thought it, though.'

She looked at him for several thoughtful minutes before answering. 'No. No, I haven't.'

Linus really was going to shake her in a minute! Although he doubted that touching Andi at the moment, even to shake her, was a good idea…

This situation was damned frustrating, though—like conversing with a block of wood. Except this block of wood looked and sounded like Andi. The woman he had made love with two evenings ago.

'I'll bring the sorted post through to you in a few minutes,' Andi told Linus pointedly as he continued to stand beside her desk.

She had thought long and hard during the night about how she should approach seeing Linus again this morning, and had finally decided that the best way to deal with the situation was to come into work at her usual time. The fact that she had instantly felt defensive the moment Linus had entered her office, felt her outward demeanour becoming stiffly distant and cool, hadn't been planned at all. It had just happened.

Andi had lain in bed the night before considering the possibilities, but no matter how hard she'd tried she hadn't been able to arrive at a believable reason as to why Linus had returned from Scotland so suddenly. Lots of unbelievable ones, but none that she could actually accept as being true. His mood this morning—terse and impatient—wasn't conducive to asking him about it, either.

'Linus…?' she prompted again as he made no move to go through to his own office.

'Yes. Fine.' After one last, irritated glance, he turned abruptly on his heel and went through to the adjoining room.

Andi's breath left her in a relieved sigh as soon as the door had been closed between the two of them. Although she instantly tensed again when she heard the loud string of oaths coming from Linus's office only seconds before the door between them was thrown open again, and he marched furiously across the room to confront her across her desk.

'What is this?' He waved a sheet of notepaper in front of her face.

Andi looked from the letter back up into Linus's furious face. 'It appears to be my letter of resignation.'

'*Appears* to be?' he rasped. 'You know damn well that it is! I thought we were going to talk about this before you decided on anything, Andi?' He glared down at her between narrowed lids, a nerve pulsing in his clenched jaw.

Andi shrugged, hoping that none of her inner trepidation was evident on her face. She really hadn't expected Linus to react so violently to her resignation. After all, it was freeing him from an embarrassing situation as much as it was her.

As hard as she tried—as much as she wanted to—Andi couldn't see any other alternative to ending this awkward situation. 'I've given you the required three months' notice, Linus.' She frowned. 'I will, of course, be more than happy to train up my replacement during that—'

'There isn't going to *be* a replacement, damn it!' he bit out.

'You no longer require a PA…?' she said doubtfully. Linus was brilliant at what he did, but he had far too many business interests nowadays to be able to deal with all of them capably, as well as deal with the minutiae of that business life.

Linus stared down at her in frustration. 'I'm refusing to accept your resignation.'

'You can't refuse, Linus.' Andi stood up to face him indignantly. 'An employer can't refuse an employee's resignation. It just isn't done.'

'No?' he challenged tauntingly. 'Well, I've just done it!' As if to prove his point, he ripped her letter into eight neatly square pieces before dropping it into the bin beside her desk. 'You aren't leaving, Andi,' he assured her firmly. 'You're going to stay right here so that we can sort this situation out. To both our satisfactions.'

She eyed him uncertainly now. 'I am…?'

'Yes. You are.' Linus moved to sit on the side of her desk. 'Did you talk to Marjorie last night?'

Andi's expression at once became guarded. 'Yes, I did.'

'And…?'

'And it would appear that my taste in men has always been flawed,' she acknowledged self-effacingly.

His gaze narrowed. 'Are you including me in that sweeping statement?'

Andi looked startled. 'No, of course not! I was referring to my first date at the burger takeaway, so that Phil could crib from my notes, and my equally stupid naivety concerning David's motives for wanting to marry me.'

Linus's expression softened as he saw the hurt and bewilderment she had been hiding from him earlier. 'I happen to like that slight naivety in you,' he murmured throatily.

Andi swallowed hard. 'You do?'

He nodded slowly. 'I do. Andi, your taste in men isn't flawed,' he continued firmly. 'You just happen to have had the bad luck to be involved with at least two men who took advantage of the fact that you trusted them.'

She gave a self-disgusted grimace. 'That still doesn't explain why I didn't see—I'm so ashamed that I didn't realize that my mother was keeping something from me all this time.'

Linus stood up. 'You weren't supposed to realize, Andi,' he comforted gently. 'Marjorie was just doing what mothers do—protecting her child from being hurt any more than she needed to be,' he explained at Andi's pained expression.

'You realized it was all a lie.'

Linus looked at her searchingly, wondering what Andi's feelings were now that she knew the truth. Apart from self-disgust, Linus could read nothing from her expression. 'It was easier for me when I wasn't close to the situation like you were.' He shrugged. 'Andi, how do you feel about Simmington-Browne now?'

Her smile was rueful. 'The same way I've always felt.'

'You're still in love with him?' Linus gasped disbelievingly. 'Even knowing the truth about him?'

Andi looked at him from beneath lowered lashes. No matter what Linus said to the contrary, she would be leaving his employment, either today or in three months' time. Far better to have the air cleared between them than to leave any misunderstandings.

She gave a dismissive shake of her head even as she raised her chin defensively, her gaze clear and steady as it met Linus's searching one. 'I never loved David, Linus. I thought I did. I was dazzled by him. Flattered by his attentions. But, even before my mother told me the truth about him, I had realized that I'd never been in love with him.'

'I—but— Then what the hell has the last few days been about?' Linus scowled at her.

'Exactly that.' Andi gave a small smile.

Linus became very still. 'You realizing you didn't love Simmington-Browne, after all?'

'Basically, yes.'

Linus looked at her searchingly, at that cool, clear brow. The dark depths of her eyes, the tiny, slightly uptilting nose. At her perfect bow of a mouth. The stubborn curve of her chin.

'Andi, why have you handed in your notice?'

She gave a shrug. 'You said we had two options—' She broke off to look at Linus with puzzled eyes as his hand reached out, and he curved his fingers about her arm as she would have moved away from him. 'Linus…?' Her expression was one of uncertainty.

Linus had driven back from Scotland the day before as if the devil were at his heels. Or as if he'd half-expected Andi to have already flown before he could reach Tarrington Park. As it turned out he'd actually got back before her, managing to extract a promise from Marjorie that she wouldn't allow Andi to leave without seeing him again. If Marjorie had guessed the reason for his determination to speak to Andi today, then she hadn't said anything. Hadn't questioned him.

He was no good at this, Linus realized disgustedly. He had no experience on which to draw. Had no idea where to even start!

His thumb moved caressingly against the

pulse that throbbed in the delicacy of Andi's wrist as he spoke huskily. 'Andi, I don't want you to leave.'

She shook her head, lashes downcast, making it impossible for Linus to read the expression in her eyes. 'I can't become your mistress, Linus.'

'I don't want you to be my mistress.'

'But you said—'

'I know what I said,' he muttered wretchedly. 'I was an idiot.'

She gave a tremulous smile even as she shook her head. 'We can't continue working together, either, after—after what happened.'

'I don't give a damn whether we continue working together or not!' Linus scowled darkly. 'I would prefer that we did, of course, but if you feel that we can't then I'll accept your decision.'

'There's nothing more to talk about, then.' She pulled abruptly out of his grasp and moved sharply away from him to move over to the window, standing with her back towards him.

'Andi…'

'Could we please not talk about this any more, Linus?' she interrupted forcefully. 'I can't— I would rather—' Andi gave a shake of her head, blonde hair moving silkily about her shoulders. 'Would you just go back to your own office, Linus?' she requested emotionally.

Linus crossed the room in two long strides, his hands coming down gently on Andi's shoulders as he pulled her back against him. She felt so good, the curve of her back and bottom fitting snugly into his chest and thighs. 'I'm in love with you, Andi,' he muttered huskily, his lips against the warmth of her temple as he felt her stiffen. 'I'm so much in love with you, I can't think straight.' His hands tightened on her shoulders. 'At least give me a chance. Let me show you how good it could be between us. I know I'm not exactly what you want, what you deserve, but at least let me try!'

Andi was stunned, shocked into silence. Hardly daring to believe...

She turned sharply in his arms, taking Linus totally by surprise; she was able to see in that moment the love shining brightly in unguarded green eyes. 'Linus!' She stared at him wonderingly.

'Are you crying?' He reached up and gently touched the wetness on her cheeks. 'I know I've bungled things between us, Andi.' He groaned, aching. 'I was wrong, offering you an affair. Don't cry, Andi,' he pleaded huskily as she began to do exactly that. 'You can leave today, if that's what you want,' he assured her. 'I won't force you to stay on here and work for me when you obviously can't even stand to be anywhere near me—'

'Linus,' Andi softly interrupted him, at the same time placing her fingertips lightly against his lips. 'You are *exactly* what I want. Exactly what I deserve,' she told him without hesitation. 'Linus, I love you too. So much, my darling. So very, very much!' She stepped completely into his arms, her own arms going about his waist as she curved her body against his and rested her head against his chest to hear the heavy throb of his heart. A heart that belonged to her.

It was unbelievable. Incredible. Wonderful!

'You love me…?' Linus seemed even less inclined to believe it than she did.

Andi looked up at him, her tears ones of happiness now. 'Of course I love you, Linus.' She smiled up at him. 'How could I not love you? You're honest. And good. And generous. And—'

'And arrogant. And dictatorial,' he reminded her with a pained wince.

Andi laughed softly. 'Only when you need to be.'

His grimace was self-mocking. 'I must need to be quite often, then!'

'Linus, if you don't kiss me soon I think I'm going to die!' Andi groaned her need.

Linus looked down at her searchingly, seeing the love shining in the glow of her eyes and the beauty of her smile. 'Before I do, Andi—neither of the options I came up with last night is acceptable to me.' His expression had darkened.

'They aren't…?' Andi's expression was once again uncertain.

Linus's arms tightened about her. 'I want to marry you, Andi. I realized exactly how I felt about you when that train drew out of the station yesterday and you told me I had to let you go. Letting you go is the very last thing I want to do. I called out to you.'

'I couldn't hear you,' she choked. 'You want to marry me, Linus?'

'More than anything else I've ever wanted. More than anything else I will ever want,' he assured her fiercely. 'Marry me, Andi. Marry me, and I promise I'll spend the rest of my life showing you how much I love you!'

'As long as I can spend the rest of my life showing you how much I love you!' Andi accepted gladly as Linus swept her tightly into his arms, and his lips at last claimed hers.

Home; Andi knew that she was home. That wherever Linus was would always be her home.

Andi's cheeks were flushed, her lips slightly swollen from their kiss, when she looked up at Linus a long time later. 'You don't want me to continue working for you after we're married?'

'I want whatever you want,' Linus assured her huskily, knowing he held all of his happiness in his arms.

Her smile was mischievous. 'I believe at the moment I would like to compare making love with you on a desk top as opposed to a table top…'

Linus returned that smile as he remembered the wildness of their love-making two evenings ago. 'Exactly the reason working together is going to be so *interesting* in future. Maybe my motives in employing Mrs Ferguson were Machiavellian, after all—because wherever I am in future, Andi, I want you at my side.'

'I won't ever want to be anywhere else,' Andi assured him huskily.

'Just think of all the places we haven't made love yet,' he mused softly.

'I am,' Andi answered teasingly. 'Oh, I assure you, I am!'

Linus gave a throaty chuckle. 'Wanton!'

'Only for you, Linus,' she told him softly. 'Only ever for you.'

Linus had been stunned when he'd made love with Andi and had discovered she was still a virgin. Stunned, and yet at the same time deeply moved by the fact. He liked the idea of being her only lover. For the rest of her life. For the rest of both their lives.

After years of avoiding involvement, any danger of ever falling in love, Linus had realized yesterday as Andi had departed on the train that she had crept into his heart while he wasn't looking. Just as he now knew that his resentment towards what he had thought of as Andi's continuing love for Simmington-Browne was based on jealousy—another emotion Linus had never experienced before.

Linus had the feeling there would be a lot of firsts in his life now that he was in love with Andi. Now that she was in love with him too. Now that she had agreed to become his wife, and agreed to stay with him, to be with him, for the rest of their lives…

EPILOGUE

'YES!' Linus, along with thousands of other Scottish fans at the Twickenham rugby ground, threw a fist up into the air in celebration of the fact that Scotland had just defeated England in their final Six Nations game. 'You don't seem too disappointed,' he prompted ruefully as he and Andi filed out of the stadium before strolling off hand in hand to where they had parked the car.

Andi gave him an indulgent smile, not in the least bothered by Scotland's victory over England. How could she be bothered by anything when she and Linus had been married for two weeks? Two wonderful, glorious weeks of working together, living together, making love together.

'I have my own reason for celebrating,' she told him enigmatically as she waited for him to unlock the car.

Linus gave her a quizzical look. 'The Wales v Ireland match at the Millennium Stadium has only just started…?'

Andi laughed huskily. 'Much as I have come to love the game of rugby the last six weeks, it really isn't my only interest,' she teased.

'Let's go home and celebrate properly!' Linus returned the love in her smile as he moved to take her in his arms. The last six weeks had been the happiest in his life, the last two especially since Andi had become his wife.

After avoiding the state of matrimony for the first thirty-six years of his life, Linus had found that he actually liked being married. That he loved being married to Andi. Loved spending his days with her. Going home with her. Spending his nights with her. Life didn't get more perfect that this!

'Not until I've told you my news.' Andi pulled back slightly to look up at him shyly. 'I'm pregnant, Linus. Six weeks' pregnant, to be exact,' she added huskily. 'If it's a girl, with your agreement, I would like to name her Flora Mae: for your mother and Aunt Mae.'

Linus gazed down incredulously at the slenderness of Andi's body. Andi was pregnant. With his child. With their child.

Life had just become more perfect.

The really were the perfect team!

* * * * *

Turn the page for an exclusive extract from:
THE SHEIKH'S FORBIDDEN VIRGIN
by
Kate Hewitt

Taken by the sheikh for pleasure—
but as his bride…?

At her coming-of-age at twenty-one, Kalila is pledged to marry the Calistan king. Scarred, sexy Sheikh Prince Aarif is sent to escort her, his brother's betrothed, to Calista. But when the willful virgin tries to escape, he has to catch her, and the desert heat leads to scorching desire—a desire that is forbidden!

Aarif claims Kalila's virginity—even though she can never be his! Once she comes to walk up the aisle on the day of her wedding, Kalila's heart is in her mouth: *who is waiting to become her husband at the altar?*

A LIGHT, INQUIRING KNOCK SOUNDED on the door, and, turning from that grim reminder, Aarif left the bathroom and went to fulfill his brother's bidding, and express his greetings to his bride.

The official led him to the double doors of the Throne Room; inside, an expectant hush fell like a curtain being dropped into place, or perhaps pulled up.

"Your Eminence," the official said in French, the national language of Zaraq, his voice low and unctuous, "may I present His Royal Highness, King Zakari."

Aarif choked; the sound was lost amid a ripple of murmurings from the palace staff, who had assembled for this honored occasion. It would take King Bahir only one glance to realize it was not the king who graced his Throne Room today, but rather the king's brother, a lowly prince.

Aarif felt a flash of rage—directed at himself. A mistake had been made in the correspondence, he supposed. He'd delegated the task to an aide when he should have written himself and explained that he would be coming rather than his brother.

Now he would have to explain the mishap in front of company—all of Bahir's staff—and he feared the insult could be great.

"Your Eminence," he said, also speaking French, and moved into the long, narrow room with its frescoed ceilings and bare walls. He bowed, not out of obeisance but rather respect, and heard Bahir shift in his chair. "I fear my brother, His Royal Highness Zakari, was unable to attend to this glad errand, due to pressing royal business. I am honored to escort his bride, the princess Kalila, to Calista in his stead."

Bahir was silent, and, stifling a prickle of both alarm and irritation, Aarif rose. He was conscious of Bahir watching him, his skin smooth but his eyes shrewd, his mouth tightening with disappointment or displeasure, perhaps both.

Yet even before Bahir made a reply, even before the formalities had been dispensed with, Aarif found his gaze sliding, of its own accord, to the silent figure to Bahir's right.

It was his daughter, of course. Kalila. Aarif had a memory of a pretty, precocious child. He'd spoken a few words to her at the engagement party more than ten years ago now. Yet now the woman standing before him was lovely, although, he acknowledged wryly, he could see little of her.

Her head was bowed, her figure swathed in a kaftan, and yet, as if she felt the magnetic tug of his gaze, she lifted her head and her eyes met his.

It was all he could see of her, those eyes; they were almond-shaped, wide and dark, luxuriously fringed, a deep, clear golden brown. Every emotion could be seen in them, including the one that flickered there now as her gaze was drawn inexorably to his face, to his scar.

It was disgust Aarif thought he saw flare in their golden depths, and as their gazes held and clashed he felt a sharp, answering stab of disappointment and self-loathing in his own gut.

* * * * *

Be sure to look for
THE SHEIKH'S FORBIDDEN VIRGIN
by Kate Hewitt,
available October
from Harlequin Presents®!